The EX FACTOR

The EX FACTOR

Carl Webster

Published by Webster Publishing, LLC
P.O. Box 42321
Indianapolis, Indiana 46242
www.carlwebsterbooks.com
admin@carlwebsterbooks.com

ISBN 978-0-9854454-0-9
Cover Design by Loren Jones

This is a work of fiction. Names, characters, places, and incidents either are the products of the author's imagination or are used fictitiously, and any resemblance to actual persons, living or dead, business establishments, events, or locales is entirely coincidental.

This book is dedicated to the loving memory of my father, Billy C. Webster.

Acknowledgments

I would foremost like to thank my Lord and Savior, Jesus Christ for allowing me to utilize the gifts that God has given me. I would also like to express thanks to my wonderful wife Decatur, and my children, for their understanding, and support in my pursuit of my dreams, and my life's purpose. I would also like to thank my hometown, Gary, Indiana. If it weren't for you, I wouldn't be the man that I am.

1 Tony

I slowly pulled into the stamped, concrete driveway of Karen's parents' home, and I parked the car. I could never get accustomed to seeing that enormous house. Their executive home boasted Sedona bricks and twelve-foot, white columns on the front porch, which gave the home the appearance of a miniature mansion. The bottom quarter of the home's exterior consisted of a natural stone contrast and the yard was flawlessly manicured with fresh mulch and precisely trimmed bushes. They even had one of those circular driveways with a four-car garage on the side of the home. To make matters worse, they had a brand new Mercedes that always seemed to be in the driveway whenever I came over to the home with Karen to visit. If I didn't know better, I would think that Karen's father was trying to tell me something. He had spent over forty-plus years working in the Ford plant over on the east side of Indianapolis. He had made some smart investments, saved his money well and was now retired with a large cushion of money to keep him and Karen's mother very comfortable for the rest of their retired lives. He was a true illustration that a hard-working, blue-collar guy could live just as well as a corporate guy.

Karen's father always had a problem with my choice of profession. He just didn't think that a car salesman could take good care of his daughter. I couldn't fault him for that hypothesis. Sometimes the money was so tight that my pockets became virgins. But I was a good salesman. As a matter of fact, I was the best car salesman that the north side BMW dealership had ever seen. I was very good at what I did. I didn't plan on doing it for the rest of my life, just until I got my landscaping business started. I was in the process of writing my business plan so that I could start shopping for small business loans and grants.

I had always had a love for landscaping. I remember when, back in the day, my father and I would work in the yard for hours. He really took pride in how our yard looked. It was more than just cutting grass and sweeping sidewalks; it was like an art to him. My father would make sure that the lawn was neatly cut and edged like a tight fade fresh out of the barber shop. Each bush had its own small, tapered afro, and every flower smiled at the sun. My father would get up every morning before work and give our lawn some kind of attention. It could be anything from watering the lawn to pulling a few weeds. He would always say, "I'm just taking care of God's earth." I really missed my dad, and working on lawns just made me feel closer to him. When I worked on a property, it almost felt as if my dad was working right next to me.

Karen must have had a long day at the firm, because she slept the entire way there. We lived only thirty minutes from her parents, but since we left during rush hour, it took us about an hour. I looked over at her sleeping in the passenger seat of the car. She looked so peaceful. Her long, black hair rested perfectly on her shoulders as if she were posing for a photograph. Her skin was a peanut butter color without a single blemish. The texture of her hair reflected her mixed heritage, due to her mother's Creole contribution. Karen had thin lips, hazel-brown eyes, and a body like Serena Williams. My girl was one of the finest, even though her mouth was wide open and she was snoring like a bear in December. We had known each other for about five years, and we had dated for three years until recently, when I popped the big question. I had to do it. Karen had been there for me through all of my misfortunes and falls.

When I first met Karen, she was just one of my dime-pieces that I would call when I needed someone to show off to the fellas. She was my show chick. You know, the girl that you take with you to cookouts, nice restaurants and Indiana Pacers games. I have to admit: she was the finest that I had ever dated, and I have dated some fine ones. Karen just really stood out from the other girls. Whenever I needed her, she was there without any questions. So there should be no question why I would be ready to take that long journey with her. Besides, she was the sexiest ball and chain that I had ever seen.

I gently touched her shoulder. "Baby, we're here. It's time to get up."

"I wasn't asleep." She opened her eyes and moved her hair out of her face. The grin that her sexy, thin lips displayed told me she was lying.

Her hypnotic eyes met mine. "How long have you been sitting here staring at me, Mr. Tony?"

I gave her a devilish grin. "About ten minutes. I've been trying to convince myself that walking with you into your parents' home would be better than me turning this car around and taking you home to do some really freaky things to you. You were looking so good over there that I almost got the steering wheel pregnant."

"You're silly. Maybe I will take you up on that offer if you behave yourself in there tonight. You can't let Daddy get to you. You just have to be the bigger man and let his words roll off your back."

4

Karen sat up and straightened her blouse. She was right. I always seemed to get into a battle of words with her father every time that I saw him. I didn't have anything against the old guy. As a matter of fact, I loved and respected him very much. He was a good man. He just liked to be right and have the final word, and I wasn't going out like that. But, I would be on my best behavior tonight, or I wouldn't get any "na-na" later on.

I turned off the car and I made my way around to Karen's side of the car. I opened her door and observed her smooth and silky legs as she positioned her body to depart from the passenger's seat of the car. As soon as Karen's Nine West pumps touched the concrete of her parents' driveway, I offered her my hand to help her out of the car. Karen adjusted her ruffled, short-sleeved blouse and her belted, twill, pencil skirt. She then ran all ten of her fingers through her hair to perk up its appearance.

Karen and I hiked up the stone porch of her parents' home and we rang the doorbell. Her mom quickly opened the door and greeted Karen with an electrifying squeeze and a kiss on her cheek. She was clearly very happy to see her only child. After the joyous reunion was over, Karen's mom then greeted me with her sweet and calming tone, and then she hugged me.

"Come in, come in. It's so good to see the two of you. How have you two been?"

"We've been great, Mom. Sorry that we are a little late, but traffic was thick on the way here."

"Oh, don't you worry about that. We're just glad the two of you found some time to share with a couple of old folks. You both look so cute together. I am so happy for you. I can't wait for you to walk down that aisle in your beautiful dress."

Karen's mom's face blushed a little as she placed her palms on both of her cheeks. She was happy that Karen and I were finally going to get married. In the middle of Karen and her mom's dialog, Karen's father entered the foyer from his office, which is located just off the entry to the home.

"Baby girl, are you telling me that you can't come in and speak to your daddy? You know that you will always be my baby girl."

Karen and her father hugged as he lifted her into the air during their embrace. As they were engaged in their father-daughter hug, Karen's father looked at me as both corners of his mouth faced the tiled floor in the foyer. Karen was a daddy's girl. She loved her father dearly. He spoiled her tremendously when she was young, and he still continued that tradition. He reached his hand out to shake mine.

"Hello, future son-in-law."

6

"Hello, sir." Karen's father squeezed my hand as hard as he could. I could actually feel the circulation in my hand screeching to a halt. All of my knuckles were forced on top of each other as the pain shot up my arm.

I refused to show him that I was in pain. I attempted to squeeze his hand with the same amount of force that he was using. That handshake had to last at least a couple of minutes. Sweat beads formed on my forehead as veins protruded from my neck. I could see the determination and focus in Karen's father's eyes as a stream of sweat trickled down the side of his face. Both of our arms were trembling as we both tried to compress each other's hand.

Our manly attempt to stake sole claim to Karen's heart was interrupted by Karen and her mom. After our two-minute handshake was cancelled, I wiggled my fingers to jump-start the circulation in my hand. Her father did the same.

"Tony, I hope that you are treating my daughter like the princess that she is. I always tell her that if she is not being treated like a princess, then she is always welcome to come back home to her original castle."

"Yes, sir. I am doing my best to treat her like a princess."

"Well, how do I know that your best is good enough for my daughter?"

"I—"

Karen's mother immediately interrupted our conversation.

"Let's all go into the dining room and eat the wonderful meal that I've prepared."

Karen gave me a look to remind me of our earlier conversation in the car and then grabbed my sore hand and escorted me to the dining room. As we entered the dining room, the aroma of the food that Karen's mom had cooked filled my nostrils. My eyes scanned the wooden dining room table to observe our prepared meal. The table was beautifully set, and there was gospel music playing softly in the background. We all took our places at the table. I sat next to Karen. Karen's dad took his seat at the head of the table. As we placed our napkins in our laps, Karen's mom scooped food onto our plates. There was baked chicken, potato salad, macaroni, and a bean casserole that her mom had made.

I was very hungry. My stomach growled as I looked over the food. I smiled as Karen's mom placed food onto my plate.

"Tony, I am going to give you lots of this bean casserole. It's a new recipe that I tried. Make sure and tell me what you think."

She piled the bean casserole onto my plate. After Karen's mom filled everyone's plate, she took her place between Karen and Karen's father. We all joined hands as Karen's father said grace.

"AMEN."

I dug in. The baked chicken was seasoned to perfection. The potato salad was mouth-watering. The macaroni was scrumptious. The bean casserole tasted like a dirty shoe. It tasted so bad that every bite left an aftertaste that the lemonade was unable to get rid of. I almost gagged when the first portion entered my mouth. I had never tasted anything so awful. I tried not to show my discontent for the bean casserole. I looked up from my plate, and Karen's father was looking directly at me. I then looked down at his plate and he only had a sample of the bean casserole. I looked over at Karen, and she had the same skimpy portion that he did. I was the only one that Karen's mom had given enough of the bean casserole to feed ten hungry kids in Africa.

Karen's father smirked. He knew that the bean casserole was terrible. I watched him shove the little bit that was on his plate into his mouth. He immediately drank half of his lemonade to flush it down his throat. He then looked over at me and smirked again.

"Tony, how is the bean casserole?"

"It's very good, sir."

I was telling a terrible lie. Karen's mom looked over at me and she smiled. I returned a smile. Karen's father then reached for the bowl of bean casserole that was in the middle of the table and handed it to Karen's mom.

"Honey, give Tony some more of your bean casserole. It looks like his plate is getting low."

Karen's mom heaped more of the horrific slop onto my plate. I tried to hold my breath as I ate it. I tried to mix it with the macaroni that was on my plate to mask the taste. I drank four glasses of lemonade to flush the bean casserole down my throat. None of this helped in disguising the unpleasant taste of the bean casserole.

I finally managed to eat my entire plate of food. After dinner, we all headed to the family room to watch a movie. I couldn't even enjoy it. That bean casserole did a number on me. The entire time, my stomach was cramping like a teenage girl on her period.

2 Tyson

What a day. Thank God it was Friday. It had really been a long week. I had been working on my presentation for my marketing approach for the Vizion Electronics account that my company recently obtained. I had been working for Von Marketing for three years, and I was in charge of creating advertising strategies for many big-name companies. As a matter of fact, many companies came to Von Marketing and asked for me personally. I'd been on a roll with my marketing skills of late. Every ad that I had created got great reviews from our bosses upstairs. People always asked me how I came up with some of the ideas that I used for my advertisements. I always gave them some high-and-mighty speech about commitment and hard work. Corporate guys liked to hear that. I told them that I stayed up late nights at home with ideas bouncing around in my head, just waiting to get to work in the morning to let them out.

The truth of the matter is, I just wrote down the first thing that popped up in my mind. When I was a kid, I would watch cartoons all day long, so I had lots of silly phrases stuck inside my memory. When it was time to brainstorm and come up with a concept for an advertisement, I'd just daydream and start writing. Luckily for me, it always made me look like a genius. I would say that the time was soon approaching for me to get some kind of raise or promotion for all my hard work.

Since I got off work a little earlier than usual that day, I decided to stop by the Slippery Noodle and have a few drinks with the after-work crowd. The Slippery Noodle is an old blues club in Indianapolis over on Meridian Street that brings in a hefty crowd on Fridays and Saturdays. During the week, they had an after-work setting from five to seven that catered to the after-work crowd. I could go and mingle with some of the most beautiful businesswomen in Indianapolis. It was a great way to relieve some of the tension that I had accumulated during my busy workday. It was also a great place for networking. I went about twice a week if my job allowed it. I had met some very interesting people in there in the past.

Once, I met this woman who worked for the state. She was well dressed in an all-navy business suit with a knee-length skirt. She had legs you would die for. They were long with defined calves. She had on a ruffled, white blouse that hugged her C-cups perfectly. Her hair was long and black and was pulled into a ponytail. I bought her a few drinks, and we talked about everything under the sun. She explained how she felt that there weren't any good men left in the world. My penis instincts kicked in, and I instantly noticed an opportunity to go in for the kill.

"Well, maybe all of the good men are not aware that there are good women as fine as yourself walking around here not being treated like you should. I'm not trying to speak game or anything, but if I had a woman like you, then I would straighten up my act immediately. You should be treated like the queen that you are. You are gorgeous and very intellectual."

She looked at me and showed some teeth. "Sometimes being gorgeous is not enough for a man. As far as men are concerned, they want a woman with a brain like they want a prostate examination. Men just want a yes-girl. Yes, you can hit it. Yes, you can go to the strip club, and, yes, you can tip a twenty-year-old stripper half your paycheck. That's why I've decided to just take it easy for a while. I need some time to find myself, and then maybe I will work on another relationship."

Ding, ding, ding! That is all I needed to hear. Without even asking, I could easily tell that she had just gotten out of a bad relationship, and she had probably been cheated on. Sometimes it is so funny how much you can learn about a person in a short conversation. I had always had a way with my words when dealing with the opposite sex. I easily convinced her to come back to my loft with me. She was all for it.

When we arrived at my loft, I instantly noticed that she was even more beautiful in the light than she was in that dark club. Once she saw how nice my loft was, I knew that I wouldn't have any trouble getting her undressed. We weren't in the loft for five minutes, and she was all over me. Her kisses were strong and passionate. When she kissed me, she grabbed the back of my head with one hand and gripped my butt with the other. She was very aggressive, but I was totally with it. I motioned her toward the stairs to my bedroom as I turned on some Mary J. Blige on my Bose 3-2-1 stereo. I couldn't wait to get up that skirt. I followed her up the stairs, and we made our way into my bedroom. I dimmed the lights just enough to make the atmosphere right, but not too dark where I couldn't observe the fine sister standing in front of me. We kissed again, while I gently removed her suit jacket and her blouse. Her breast and bra combination looked like an ad for Victoria's Secret. I slowly gripped her breasts with both of my hands and began to caress them. By the resonance of her moans and her heavy breathing, I could tell that she was totally feeling it. She started to undress me. She was biting her bottom lip the whole time and giving me a devilish grin. I smiled from ear to ear. Then, she took a step back and began to slide out of her business skirt. She did so in a sexy, hip-twisting fashion. She then slid her panties down from around her hips and eased onto my bed, still facing me. By this time, I was ready to explode like a Roman candle. I quickly began to reach for a condom inside my wallet, but I was interrupted by something that was really troubling. I sniffed both my armpits. I then blew air into my hands to test my breath. The stench wasn't coming from me. It was her. I was standing about ten feet away from this beautiful woman lying on my bed with her legs spread wide open, and I could smell her funky emotions as if they were right in front of my nose. I have smelled women's parts before, but this was not normal. The stench that I was experiencing was that of cigarettes and tuna. I almost lost my balance when the smell hit me. How could a woman so attractive be defiled with an odor that was so awful? There was no way that I was going to hit that. That thing needed to be soaked and sterilized, and I didn't think that Trojan made a Lysol-lubricated condom.

I had to get out of that situation in a hurry. I had to think fast. How in the world could I get out of having relations with her without looking like an ass-hole? I kindly excused myself and went into the hall bathroom. I used my cell phone that was in my pants pocket to call my house phone right before I came out of the bathroom. When my house phone started ring-ing, I walked over to the phone on the nightstand next to my bed, and I started talking to my imaginary friend.

"Hello? Yes, this is Tyson. He what? He did? When did this happen? No! No! Not Jimmy!"

I began to cry, and I slammed the phone down on the base. I actually produced some tears. To tell the truth, I didn't know if the tears were from my re-markable acting skills or because I really wanted to have sex with her, but she smelled like a pigpen.

"What's going on? Tyson, are you alright?"

She looked really concerned. She was starting to tear up before I even told her what happened. Maybe she should have been more concerned with the manure bag that she was packing between her legs.

I tried to speak without laughing. "It's Jimmy, my best friend's younger brother. He was hit by a car. They say it's really bad. I think I should go to the hospital and meet up with his family. They need me."

"Absolutely, I totally understand. Oh my God, I hope that he is going to be alright. Is there anything that I can do?"

I thought: *Yeah, you can go and sit in a tub filled with bleach.*

"No. Just leave me your number, and I'll call you when I make it home from the hospital. I hate to wash, I mean, watch your fine self leave, but I really should be there."

Anyway, she bought it and she left, but she left her funk behind. I didn't even try to clean those sheets. I just threw them away and sprayed my mattress with Lysol and bug spray.

***

I was interrupted from my daydream by the bright lights of downtown Meridian Street. The streets had become very busy. The sound of tires screeching, horns blaring, and engines revving filled the air. It would not take a rocket scientist to figure out that it was rush hour. I turned on the radio to try to get something playing that could ease the tension that I had accumulated during my stressful workday. Why is it that during rush hour, all you seem to find on the radio is a bunch of goofy conversations? This is the time when the DJs need to play as much music as possible. I had been hearing fake conversations all day. The last thing I wanted to do was subject myself

17

to another one. I must say, the corporate ladies were looking good tonight. Sitting at the light, watching all of those long, panty-hosed legs walking across the intersection was the highlight of rush hour. Every flavor excited me: chocolate legs, vanilla legs, and even butterscotch legs, all looking very tasty. It was enough to make a brotha's mouth water. That was a very calming sight compared to the bumper to bumper reality that I was sitting in.

3 Karen

I was so proud of Tony. I was surprised and impressed at how he behaved himself that night. He didn't add a single cent to any of Daddy's debating attempts. People really underestimate the powers that rest between a woman's thighs. You could get your man to do just about anything you want if you put it on coochie credit.

Daddy didn't mean any harm. He just wanted to make sure that I was well taken care of. Don't get me wrong, I also wanted to make sure that I was taken care of. I also knew that Tony worked very hard and that he was good at what he did. He always came home with one of those "Employee of the Month" plaques. That was just the half of it. He also got lots of Indianapolis Colts tickets and gift certificates to Red Lobster and Outback Steakhouse. The gift certificates were my favorite. He always called me from work and told me to get gorgeous so that he could take me out. He liked to see me in skirts, so I always made sure to put one on for those special occasions. Whenever he was able to take me out to one of those expensive places, he wore a glow the entire night. The expression that he kept on his face was one of pride. I swear that he smiled the entire night. Those were the nights that made me fall in love with Tony. I could really tell that he wanted the best for me. He got up for work early every morning without a single complaint. He took out the garbage without me ever asking, and he even lowered the toilet seat after he did his thing. Any man that did that was worthy of marriage. Tony even paid all the bills for our apartment. He always told me that the money I make is for me to stay pretty. He really loved it when I got my hair, feet, and hands done. Like I said before, he loved to see me in skirts, so I made sure to keep a variety of different fits and colors in stock.

Tony had been working at the car dealership for about three years. He always talked about the landscaping business that he and his father were supposed to start. Unfortunately, his father passed about five years ago. He said that he still wanted to get it started as soon as he finished working out the business plan for it. I believed in all of the dreams that Tony talked about. It was a real turn-on to hear a man speak of goals. Very few men out there had a ten-year plan. I was one of the lucky girls to have one of those men in my possession. Every place we went, Tony always said that he would like to own one of these one day. His mind was always working. He was a true businessman at heart.

Of course, I had to give Tony his reward for being on his best behavior that night. I looked over at him, sleeping like he just got home from the night shift. When a man relieves himself of his eager little swimmers, why does he curl into the fetal position like a two hundred-pound baby and hibernate? It's like one minute he was all man; then after he took a walk down the treasure trail, he turned into an instant toddler. I must admit, Tony knew his way around the bedroom. I had never known him to have to stop and ask for directions. This pirate knew how to find his gold.

My vaginal thoughts were interrupted by the sound of the phone ringing. I jumped out of bed and hurried to the kitchen to answer it so that it wouldn't wake Tony.

"Hello?" I was nearly out of breath from my sprint from the bedroom to the kitchen.

"Hey girl, what are you up to?"

"Nothing. I was just watching a little *Fresh Prince* before I go to bed."

It was my girl, Stacey. I could tell by the loud music in the background and all of the voices screaming over each other that she was probably out at the club or some kind of bar. And it wouldn't take a genius to figure out that she had been drinking. Her buzzed voice spoke into my phone.

"What are you doing getting ready for bed this early on a Friday night? Some of the players from the Pacers are throwing a party at Club Seven tonight, and ladies get in free before eleven. You need to be up here getting one of these Pacers men. They haven't arrived yet, but I'll be waiting on them when they get here."

That was Stacey, always at the club. She had this confused notion that the club or bar is where you go to meet your husband. It didn't matter the occasion. If it was a party or a get-together, Stacey was there.

"Stacey, you know that I have a man. As a matter of fact, he is more than just my man; he is my future husband. Besides, you shouldn't be wasting your time on any of those ballplayers anyway. They are not coming to that club to meet "Mrs. Right." They want to meet "Mrs. Right Now." They're just looking for some groupies that are dumb enough to get buck wild with them."

You could hear the frustration in my tone.

"Well, maybe I am just the one they're looking for, especially if it's Danny Granger. I can get as buck wild as he would like me to. Have you heard about his new contract? I might have the multimillion-dollar ass and I might not, but I think it's worth a shot."

You could tell that she was getting more wasted by the minute. It sounded like she was having a good time, too. I would have gone if she would have let me know earlier in the week, but I had planned dinner at my folks on Monday. I wouldn't have gone to meet anyone, but it would have been nice to go out and have a good time with the girls. I hadn't gone out with them in a while. Stacey was always a bucket of laughs. I have known her practically my whole life. She was always known as the party girl, and I was known as the quiet one. Stacey always had all of the popular guys. In high school, she dated everyone from the captain of the football team to the captain of the basketball team. She even dated the pitcher on the baseball team. Guys had always been attracted to Stacey. For one, her personality was a dude magnet. She was so upfront with her approach that guys had to respect it.

Stacey had dark brown hair that was cut short and tapered in the back. Her hairstyle was always flawless. Her makeup was always in good standing. She had a small waist, wide hips, and small breasts. Men always went crazy whenever Stacey wore her Apple Bottom jeans and a pair of high-heeled shoes. I swear, she probably had those jeans in every color.

"I guess I can't argue with that. Well, I'm going to let you get back to your Pacers, and I'm going to go and lay next to my Seventy-Sixer, if you know what I mean."

"You wish. Bye,girl."

"Be careful. Bye."

I hung up the phone and headed back to the bedroom to lie next to my hibernating man.

4 Tony

I got up early this morning and headed to the gym to meet up with Jay. We went there before work about three times a week to get a good workout. Jay was a real workout junkie. He worked out faithfully. He drank those energy drinks and watched what he ate all the time. *Nothing but fish and chicken. Baked not fried.* Those were the famous words he uttered every time we grabbed a bite to eat. He was cool people, though. We had been good friends for about ten years. He worked at the same car lot that I did. Jay was actually the one who referred me to my supervisor for a sales position. He had worked at the lot two years before I started.

Jay and I started running on the treadmill. I always ran on the treadmill right after I stretched, when we first arrived at the gym. I liked to get my heart rate up so that I could get motivated for the weightlifting portion of our workout. We quickly claimed the two treadmills in the front corner of the gym. I liked to use those because they were located directly underneath one of the plasma televisions that hung from the ceiling of the gym. I guess that you could call our workouts a form of male bonding. We ran on the treadmills next to each other as we watched the highlights on SportsCenter and didn't say a word to each other the entire time. We both had our MP3 players blasting our own music of choice into our ears. Every now and then, I would look over at the screen on Jay's treadmill to see if he was running as fast as I was. If he was, then I would crank up the speed on my treadmill to prove that I was in better shape. This time, I noticed that he was running at a 6.0 pace, so I adjusted my pace to 6.3. We went through that same scenario about five times before we finished our treadmill run.

After about forty-five minutes on the tread-mills, we did some stretches, and then we headed over to the free-weights. It was our day to work on our biceps and triceps. Jay walked over from the water fountain and motioned for us to do curls first. He smirked.

"So, are you going to work out for real this time, or are you going to punk out like the last time. You were barely able to complete the workout."

"What are you talking about? I was lifting more weight than you were. You should have been able to work out for hours. I think I saw a soccer mom lifting the same amount of weight that you were." I smiled, proud of my comeback.

Jay quickly changed the subject.

"So, I noticed that you were ranked number two this month so far in sales. Guess who is ranked number one?"

I laughed. "It's probably the same person who will be ranked number two by the end of the month."

We competed in everything. It didn't matter what it was. If Jay could do it, then I could do it better, and vice versa. If I pulled up to work in the morning and my car was clean and Jay's wasn't, then he would take his car to the carwash on his lunch hour. You should have seen us while we were at work. When a potential customer got out of her car, we were both falling over desks and garbage cans inside the building, trying to be the first one outside to greet her. People always asked us if we were brothers. Neither one of us had any siblings, so I guess that was where all of the competitiveness between us came from.

We continued to lift weights as we went on with our banter. Sometimes all of the laughing made it difficult for me to lift the heavy dumbbells.

"What did you do after work last night?"

"Karen and I went over to her parents' house to have dinner."

"Sounds like another day in the life of being on lockdown."

Jay always gave me a hard time about being in a serious relationship. He was a self-proclaimed ladies' man.

"You are on a roll this morning. I assume that your night was more interesting than mine was."

"Actually, it was. I wasn't planning on doing anything last night. I was very tired from outselling you on the car lot all day. All I wanted to do was come home, eat, and watch the Pacers play the Lakers on television. As soon as I got home from work, Tammy called me."

"You mean crazy Tammy with the light eyes?"

"That's the one."

"I thought that you were done with her."

"Well, I was. At least I thought I was. She called me and asked me if she could come over. I really didn't feel like entertaining last night, so I thought I would have a little fun."

"What do you mean?"

"Well, like I said before, the Pacers were playing the Lakers last night. I told Tammy that if she'd bring me something to eat while I watched the game, she was welcome to watch it with me."

"So, what was wrong with that?"

"Slow down. I'm getting to it. I told her that she was welcome to come over and watch the game with me, but she would have to leave after it was over, unless the Pacers won. The Lakers were at 12-1 for the season. I figured there was no way the Pacers would beat them. By making the bet, I figured that I could get some free food out of the deal and not have to spend very much time with her."

"That's cold."

"I know. Man, I wish you could have seen her. She came over to my apartment and brought me some wings from Hooters. We started to watch the game, and she was totally into it. Tammy was cheering for every basket that the Pacers made. She was folding her hands together and saying a silent prayer every time one of the Pacers' players was on the free-throw line. Tammy sat on the edge of the couch for the entire game. It was hilarious."

"You have no conscience."

"Everything was going good for me. The Lakers had a fifteen-point lead going into the fourth quarter. Then, all of a sudden, the Pacers went on a scoring spree. Everything they threw into the air was falling for them. Both Tammy and I were screaming at the top of our lungs. It came down to the very last second. The Lakers were up by one point with twenty-six seconds left. Kobe shot a jumper and missed it.

The Pacers got the rebound with only twelve seconds on the clock. Danny Granger shot a jumper and missed it off the left side of the rim. Everyone was fighting for the rebound when, out of nowhere, Murphy tipped the ball into the basket for the Pacers as the clock ran out. The Pacers ended up winning by one point."

"That is hilarious."

"I know. She was very excited. She was jumping up and down and celebrating her victory all over my apartment. Needless to say, I kept my word, and I allowed her to spend the night with me."

"Oh, how honorable of you. I'm sure that she made it worth your while."

"She sure did."

Jay had us doing every bicep and triceps exercise he could think of. At the end of our workout, we both walked to the parking lot, trying to hide the pain that we were both experiencing from the grueling workout. My arms were on fire, and my legs felt limp. I really regretted turning the speed up so high on that treadmill.

"What do you have going on tonight after work?"

Jay wiped his brow with his sweat towel.

"Nothing really. I was planning on going home and working on this business plan a little before Karen gets home from work."

I liked to get all of my errands and projects done before Karen got home so that we could spend some quality time together. When you have a woman as special as the one that I had, you have to put in some extra time to keep her happy. She worked long days and was usually both mentally and physically drained by the time she got home. I tried to have a tub filled with warm water and bubbles waiting for her when she got home. Today, I thought, I would pour in a little of that Sweet Pea body splash that she bought from Bath & Body Works. I really liked the way it smelled on her skin. While I was at it, I thought to myself, I might even pick her out something sexy to wear to bed tonight. Hell, I might as well make it a freaky night.

"I guess that means that you're on lockdown tonight, huh? That girl got your balls in a pink pair of pliers." Jay started to laugh uncontrollably. "I was going to invite you to watch the Pacers game tonight on my new plasma television," he continued, "but I see that the lives of your future children are at risk."

I tried not to laugh. "Your jokes get worse by the minute. I'm just trying to keep the peace in my household. As long as my lady is happy, then the whole house is happy."

Jay wiped his brow again. "Hey, you better watch out getting close to these women and putting everything that you have into these relationships. It seems like as long as you act as if you don't care about a woman, then everything is fine. The minute they see you're really in it for the long haul and that you've fallen for them, they start to act up. No more cooked meals, no clean house and, worst of all, no more playtime before bedtime."

"I am a grown man. I think that I have enough experience to know how to treat a woman. When you have been dealing with all of the hoochies that you always deal with, then of course you're going to run into some turbulence. I think that I can roll my own dice with this one, but thanks for the advice."

We both started to laugh and walked toward our own cars. Jay looked over at me from across the lot before he opened his car door, and he yelled at the top of his lungs: "Get your balls back!"

I couldn't even reply. Everyone that was outside in the parking lot stopped what they were doing and looked over at us. I tried to hurry up and get into my car before anyone realized that it was me that he was talking to.

5 Karen

It was Monday again. I was a little upset when I came to work this morning. As soon as I entered my work area, my supervisor informed me that I had been moved to another creative team. I had been working on my current team for almost a year, and I was really starting to make progress. I was becoming one of the most recognized individuals on the team and was actually next in line for a promotion. Every time that our team had a meeting with one of the managers or with one of our clients, I was always the spokesperson. I was the point of contact for all of our clients.

Now that I was on a different team, I would be last in line for a promotion on this new team. It was almost like starting all over again. An entire year of building my brand was down the drain in a matter of minutes. I guess that's how it goes in corporate America.

When I entered the conference room to meet my new team, it was a little uncomfortable at first.

The team member that I was replacing was let go because of a lack of production. I was filling some very small shoes. At least it would not be a problem to show how productive I could be. A very hard worker, I took my career very seriously. I liked to be the leader in the group. I liked to be the one who took control of the meetings.

Very early in the introduction of my team members, I learned that I would have some competition. The other two individuals on my team were easily tamed, but the third was one to be concerned about. Self-assured and well dressed, he was very smooth and well-informed with a sexy bald head and dark eyebrows. His skin was caramel colored, and he had a sporty build. You could easily see that he had worked very hard to get to where he was, and he had no intention of giving up his secure place on the team. He was clearly the all-star of this team—kind of like what I was on my last team.

He approached me and extended his hand.

"Hello, Karen. It is a pleasure to meet you. We have all heard so much about you and your great performance on the other team that you were on. My name is Tyson Smith, and this is Kathy Wright and John Kingston." His handshake was firm, yet gentle. He was a very articulate man.

I smiled. "Hi, Tyson. It's nice to meet you. And it is also very nice to meet the both of you as well. I am honored to be a new addition to this already very successful team."

I had to butter them up a little. This business, like many other businesses, was all about politics. It was all about *who* you knew and not *what* you knew. It was okay to step on a few toes on your way to the top, but you couldn't burn any bridges. The very person you didn't get along with on your last team could very well be the manager you answered to in a few months.

Tyson was a cool guy. He was kind of full of himself, and I noticed he was somewhat of a ladies' man. Tyson wore a chocolate-brown, tailored suit with a sky-blue dress shirt and blue tie to match. His hands were strong but well taken care of. No dirt under the fingernails. He had on brown Kenneth Cole dress shoes, and his cologne was noticeable but not excessively strong. Tyson's breath smelled like mints and coffee, and he kept strong eye contact while he spoke to me. He was the kind of guy that mothers warn their daughters about. But he was also the kind of guy that makes you want to ignore your mother's wisdom and date him anyway. He looked and sounded very professional.

Tyson was very different from my man. Tony was more of a blue-collared man, like my father. I loved those types—the type of man who isn't scared to get his hands dirty. My man worked his fingers to the bone for me. Nothing is sexier, I thought, than a man after he has just washed the car or cut the lawn— his face covered in sweat, his T-shirt drenching wet. I didn't want a man who took his car to the car wash or paid one of the neighborhood kids to cut the lawn. I preferred my man to have a hammer in one hand and a paycheck in the other. Just the thought of my man made me moist. *I might have to head home early today*, I thought. *Maybe I'd just call him and give him a few hints as to what he could expect from me tonight. I might even wear one of my killer bra-and-panty combinations for him.* I had the perfect set in mind. I had just bought a black bra and panty set from Victoria's Secret. Tony always told me that he liked the way black looked against my skin. *I could even throw on my new pair of black, four-inch heels that I just bought from DSW. Then, I could put my hair up in a ponytail and put on my reading glasses. That way, I could look like one of his teachers that he probably fantasized about when he was in school. Yes, I'd give him the business tonight. I hoped that he didn't overdo it at the gym with Jay because he would need some endurance to keep up with me tonight.*

6 Tyson

I could already tell that the new girl we just added to our team at work was going to be a problem. I had heard about how good she was on her previous team. Well, this was my team, and I wasn't down for a Kobe-and-Shaq situation. The last thing I needed was some big-shot chick setting up roadblocks to keep me from getting my next raise and promotion.

I couldn't lie; she was fine, though. I didn't know what she was mixed with, but whatever it was, I liked it. I had noticed her at work before. Sometimes she wore her hair straight like an ebony Pocahontas, and sometimes she wore it wavy. Her whole look was about the sexiest that I had seen in a long time. Her legs were beautiful. They were outlined with small ankles and calves that would drive any man crazy. She had a face like an angel and legs like a track star. *I wouldn't mind having her run a few laps with me around my bedroom.*

When I spoke to her that morning, I noticed an engagement ring on her finger. I hadn't noticed it on her before. To tell the truth, I didn't think that I had ever been close enough to her to see it. Well, somebody did the right thing to snatch her up. You could easily see that she was not like the other women around the office. Karen carried herself with pride and class. When I looked at her, I didn't see a woman that I would just like to sleep with and then avoid for the next few days so that she didn't get too attached. I saw a woman that I would sex like never before. I would hit it like it was the last piece on earth. I would actually consider foreplay with her. That's right, I said foreplay. I would really want to make myself memorable with her. I would make it a night that she would never forget. Not only would I call her the next day, but I would call her cell phone from mine immediately after we had had sex, while we were still lying next to each other.

I hoped that her man was treating her right. If not, then I might have to step in and be a substitute lover or something. He was probably not hitting it like he should anyway. I was going to keep my eye on her.

***

I just got word that our team had been assigned the new Weber Grille account, a franchise that had just opened a new location here in Indianapolis. This was great for exposure. I had eaten at the Chicago Weber Grille before. It was a classy spot. No one else on my team knew about the account yet, but our manager was planning on telling us tomorrow. The only reason I even knew about it was because I dated a chick in the accounting department about a year ago. She always gave me good information from time to time, in addition to other perks. I was going to get a jump start on some research so that I could have an advantage over the rest of the team. I even thought of some good marketing strategies that night so that I could fake like I just came up with them in our meeting the next morning. I could feel my pockets expanding already.

After I leave here this evening, I am going to head straight home and get started on developing some ideas for the campaign. I can't wait until I get all of the creative juices flowing. I have to send this babe a message. Let her know who the man is around here. I can't forget to stop and get my car washed on my way home. It is about two weeks overdue.

7 Tony

I was on fire today. I sold three cars in a little over five hours. I was really feeling it today. It just seemed as if everyone that I talked to today was really serious about buying a car. The best part about it was that one of the cars I sold was a brand new BMW 760. I couldn't wait to get paid next week. If I kept this up, then I'd be employee of the month again when this month was over. I was sure that Jay would try to make it interesting. Every time that I thought the title was in the bag, Jay went on his selling spree and tried to make a record-setting comeback. We were, by far, the best salesmen on the lot.

After we completed our shifts at the car lot, Jay persuaded me into going to Champ's downtown on Washington Street to watch the game. *Monday Night Football* had always been a popular event at Champ's. It really brought in a good crowd. On a normal day, I might not have gone, but since I was in a good mood, I happily accepted. We got to Champ's at about nine o'clock. The game had already started, but we only missed about six minutes of the first quarter. The Green Bay Packers were playing the Denver Broncos. This was glorified to be a big game because Brett Favre always put up great numbers on *Monday Night Football*. I wasn't a Packers fan or a Broncos fan, but I really enjoyed watching legends like Favre at work. My team was the Indianapolis Colts, of course. They had beat up on the Carolina Panthers yesterday. As soon as we got to the restaurant, we ordered our drinks. My mouth had been watering for a Corona all day. Jay ordered a Jack and Coke. We ended up sitting at the bar because the place was so full. I didn't mind at all. The closer to the drinks we were, the better off I was. Jay looked around the room like a man on a mission.

"There are some fine-looking women in here tonight."

I had to agree with him. I didn't know what it was about *Monday Night Football* events. It seemed as if all the beautiful women that are hiding out all weekend wait until Monday to come out and play. I smiled a devilish grin and pointed toward a table across the room.

I said to Jay, "Why don't you go over there and work your game? You claim that you are a world-class player, but I haven't seen any confirmation of that yet. If I didn't know any better, I'd think you were a fraud."

I knew this would pump Jay up to go over to the table of ebony goddesses and get embarrassed. It worked every time. Jay couldn't turn down a challenge. I had challenged his manhood. He *had* to answer. It's called "Man Law."

"How you gonna go and try to punk me like that? You know I got game. I have had some of the best eye candy that you have ever seen."

He had a real serious look on his face when he made that statement. He even sat up straight on his bar stool and used his thumb and index finger to hold open one of his eyes as a visual display.

We laughed long and hard. As soon as we were done laughing, Jay immediately hopped off the bar stool and pimped over to the table of ebony goddesses. I knew that I could talk him into it. Like I said before, "Man Law."

While Jay was over at the ebony-goddess table getting his feelings hurt, I continued to watch the game. Favre was really having a good night. I swear that he has a rocket for a throwing arm. I motioned the bartender to send over another Corona. This one had a lime in it. I immediately took the lime off the lip of the bottle and tossed it on the bar in front of me. No fruit in my beer for me. Whoever thought of putting a fruit slice in a bottle of beer must have had on pink tube socks when he came up with that idea. I took a long drink from my bottle. This second bottle of Corona was much better than the first one.

"Excuse me, Miss." I raised my hand to get the waitress' attention. She had a short frame with thin legs. She was wearing blue denim shorts that hugged her hips. She also had on a red T-shirt that stopped just below her belly button, and her name tag said "Carey." As she walked over to the side of the bar where I was sitting, she smiled and lit up the room.

"What can I get for you, Sir?"

I smiled and looked at her name tag. "Hello, Carey. I was wondering if I could get a small order of Buffalo wings."

She smiled and scribbled on her notepad.

"Would you like some ranch on the side with that?"

"You were reading my mind exactly. And while we're at it, can you bring me another cold beer?"

She smiled and headed for the kitchen. She was either one of the sexiest women I had seen in a while, or the beer was really doing her justice. As she was walking away, Jay was making his way back to the bar. His look told me that his conversation with the ebony goddesses didn't go as planned. I was all set to really give him a hard time about it. I laughed as he approached.

"No dice, huh?"

He looked over at the bartender and motioned for another Jack and Coke. "You'll never guess who was at the table I just left."

His expression was not the playful one that he had when he first headed over to the table. Jay almost looked as if he had seen a ghost or something. I looked over toward the direction of the table, but I was unable to see it due to the number of people that had crowded inside the restaurant.

I looked back at Jay. "Who was at the table that got you walking like you got your tail between your legs?"

Jay took a sip of his Jack and Coke. "It was Laura."

I could not believe my ears. We both sat there in silence for about two minutes. I don't think I blinked even once. My chest began to feel tight, and my palms began to sweat. I took a drink of my beer like it was the last one in the restaurant.

Laura was my girlfriend before Karen. I dated her for almost six years until she moved to Texas. She was offered a big office position at Verizon. We were having a few problems before the position became available for her. When Laura left for Texas, I had mixed emotions about it all. I was confused about the whole love thing. I figured that if she really loved me like she claimed she did, then Texas would not have even been an option. I mean, don't get me wrong, I did not expect her to throw her life away to be with me. But she also had a few offers on the table here in Indianapolis that were just as good and that paid just as much, if not more. Besides, I'd had plenty of chances to move in the past. I had relatives and friends all over the country. Never once did I consider leaving her and, if I did move, I would have taken her with me. She didn't even offer. As you can see, the whole experience hit me pretty hard. I was messed up for months. Laura was my rib. I would have done anything for her.

It played out like a scene in a movie. She stopped at the car lot on her way to the airport before she left. We just stood there, staring at each other. Both of us had tears in our eyes. I was speechless. I assumed that she was the same because she didn't say anything either. We kissed one last time, and that was the last time I had seen her. I watched the cab pull off, and I stared blankly as it headed down Keystone Avenue. We spoke on the phone a few times that year after she got settled in Texas, but things were different.

What was she doing here? It took some time for me to get over her, and I had finally moved on. So, why was my heart pounding this hard? Why did I have cramps in my abdomen? Maybe she didn't know that I was in here. Hopefully, Jay didn't tell her that he was in here with me.

Jay took a sip of his Jack and Coke. "I told her that you were in here with me."

Damn! What would possess him to do that? As we were talking, I noticed Jay looking past me at something. He serenely grabbed his drink and walked over to another table full of ladies. Someone tapped me on the shoulder. I didn't have to be a palm reader in order to know who it was. Besides, I could smell her fragrance before she even touched me. Just the smell of that fragrance ignited my senses and brought back memories. For a while, right after she left for Texas, I could be in the mall or at the movies, and I would smell that whiff and turn around to see if it was her. But now it wasn't some stranger at the movies who happened to wear the same perfume as she did. It was Laura herself. I turned around on my bar stool to face her.

8 Tony

Laura looked at me and gave me her heart-stopping smile. "Hello, stranger. How have you been?"

She opened her arms to hug me. I stepped down off my comfortable bar stool and wrapped my happily engaged arms around her.

"Hey…I've been doing fine. How have you been?"

"I'm doing well also. It's good to see you again."

She was looking good. I had not seen her in about six years, and she looked just as sexy as she did when she left. I never considered Laura beautiful. I always kept her in the "very pretty" category. Don't get me wrong; Laura was extremely pretty. But, as far as sexy goes, she was the sexiest woman on this planet. There is a difference between beautiful and pretty. When a woman is beautiful, she is nearly flawless. A beautiful woman is not one that you see every day. In my mind, beautiful could be best described as natural and not needing much makeup. When a woman is pretty, her makeup is on point, her hair is done up in the best style that she can afford, and her hands and feet have a fresh manicure and pedicure. These combinations all work together to contribute to "very pretty." Clothes can also aid in the completion of the "very pretty" category.

Now, sexy on the other hand is an entirely different category. You can't teach sexy. You can't wear sexy. You can't buy sexy. Sexy just *is*. Sexy is an aura. It is how a woman carries herself. It is the way a woman's lips seduce you while she speaks. It's in a woman's walk and speech. You can see sexy in a woman's eyes and even in the way she eats. Sexy is natural. Sexy can't be trained. It can't be faked. That is what Laura was. She was sexy as hell.

I looked into her mesmerizing eyes. Those round, brown eyes still calmed my core. I smiled.

"So, what brings you to Indy? Are you on vacation or something?" I asked.

She smiled back at me as if she had read my thoughts.

"No, I'm not on vacation. I have been back in Indianapolis for about a year now. Verizon offered me a position here, and since I already know lots of people from having lived here before, I accepted it. I would have called you to let you know, but the number that I had for you doesn't work anymore. I was hoping that I would eventually run into you. When I saw Jay, the first thing that I asked him was if you were here…"

She was smiling the entire time that she was talking to me. I could easily tell that she was thrilled to see me. During all of the excitement, I had almost forgotten that I was getting married. I had to tell her. I didn't want to send any mixed messages. I loved my girl. She had been there for me through some tough times. I would never do anything to jeopardize my relationship with her.

Laura parted her mouth to speak again. "I heard about your father passing away. I was shocked to hear that. I really felt bad about the whole thing. You know that I would have called you if I still had your number at the time."

I saw the look of concern in her eyes. Laura knew firsthand how close my dad and I were.

"Yeah, a lot happened while you were gone. My dad's passing really hit me hard. I still think about him from time to time. I don't think that I will ever recover from that. And you don't have to explain anything. I know that you would have been the first one to call me to console me if you had my number."

Laura gave me a childlike smile and gently placed her hand on top of mine. I could feel the warmth from her body running from my fingertips to my armpits. She glanced at my left hand.

"Well, I see that some lucky woman hasn't snatched you up and married you yet. What else is going on? Get me caught up on all of the great things happening in Tony's life."

I smiled awkwardly.

"Well, it's funny you should mention that. I am actually engaged now."

I could see the shock in her expression. Embarrassed, she pulled her hand off mine. It was probably one of the most uncomfortable moments of my life. It seemed as if everything went silent in the room at that very moment. I think the players on the television stopped moving also. Spilled drinks stopped in mid-air, just before hitting the ceramic tiles. It felt like Laura and I were the only people in the room. Just us and that word hovering above our heads: *Engaged*. I think I heard my voice crack as I said it.

Laura finally broke the silence. "That's great. I am happy for you. I'm sure that whoever it is that you chose to be your wife is a wonderful person. You really deserve it."

I thanked her and instantly tried to change the subject. We talked for over an hour. Laura told me about how much she liked living in Texas. She told me about her job and her condo that she still owned in Texas, but was currently renting out. She even told me about a few of the boyfriends that she has had while she was there. I was sure that under normal circumstances, she would not have brought up the boyfriends, but the whole engagement thing probably gave her more assurance to do it. I actually enjoyed talking to her. It was good to hear about her new life. It was also good to be able to tell her about Karen. I was glad that I was man enough to let her know before she got the wrong signals.

It was getting late, so we started to bring our conversation to a close. Laura eased off her bar stool in front of me.

"Tony, it was nice seeing you. I am really glad that I ran into you. I really enjoyed our talk. Like I said earlier, I don't have your new number, and I don't want to disrespect your girl by taking it now. So, here is my number. You can call me if you like. I'm not hitting on you, but I would love to talk to you again on a friend level like we did tonight."

I smiled and accepted the phone number that she had written on a napkin as she was talking to me. We hugged, I inhaled her fragrance, and we said our good-byes. I watched her as she walked away from where I was sitting.

I was about five seconds into my stare when Jay hopped onto the bar stool where Laura was just sitting. He didn't even speak. He just laughed, shook his head back and forth, and took a sip from his glass.

9 Karen

Work, work, work! Where do I even start? Ever since my team had taken on this new client, we had been working our butt cheeks off. It was a madhouse at the office. Everyone was working franticly, trying to stay on schedule. It really started to affect my personal time. Even when I wasn't at work, I was working. I got calls well into the night about this project.

I had gotten to know Tyson very well over the past few days due to the frequency of our work-related phone conversations. Both of us had been coming up with some great ideas for the marketing of Weber Grille. Tyson was really good; he had a brilliant imagination. We were faced with obstacles on a daily basis, but he always delivered. Our team had been spending a lot of time together. We even ate lunch together. That way, we could go over some objectives while we fed our faces. It was not uncommon to see me in a restaurant with a bagel in one hand, a pen in the other, and my cell phone wedged between my shoulder and my ear.

I rarely got home by six anymore. I was usually home by seven or eight. By the time that I did get home, I was so tired that I couldn't even stay up very long. I hadn't been able to spend very much time with Tony since my new change at work. I really felt bad about it. I tried to talk to him and watch a little television with him, but I usually fell asleep halfway into the program. When I was awake at home, my company cell phone rang continuously. I could tell that it kind of annoyed Tony, but he never said anything about it. He had been really supportive during my transition at work. Tony always told me that working this hard would pay off in the end. I sure hoped that it did. I could have really used a raise. I didn't want my parents to pay for my wedding, so Tony and I had to save up some money in order to make it happen. Maybe when I did get that big raise, I would put some money away for us to go on a cruise or something.

We could both benefit from a vacation. Lately I had noticed a change in his personality. I could tell that there were some things on his mind. It started around the time that things changed at work for me. He didn't seem angry or anything. He just seemed different. I sometimes caught him staring at the wall, deep in thought. He even made love to me differently. It was almost as if he was just going through the motions. He just didn't seem to be into it. I could even feel him tossing and turning in his sleep at night. I knew that this was taking a toll on him. But he would never say anything to me about it. That just wasn't his style. He had never been much of a complainer.

I hadn't spent any time with Stacey lately, either. We usually went out once or twice a month, but things had been so hectic lately that I just didn't have the time. My work life was really taking a toll on my private life. The bad thing about it was, I had asked for it. Well, the career part, of course. I had waited so long for the opportunity to take my career to that next level. I had gotten a lot of exposure working on this project. All of the big names of our company had an eye on us because of the scope of this project. We *had* to pull this off. This *had* to be a success.

I often wondered if everyone with a demanding, respectable career was experiencing the same issues that I was. Was this the life that I prayed for all these years? I loved the work that I did. I loved my position, even though I wanted a higher one. I was really good at what I did. I even loved the company that I worked for. But I also loved my man. He had been there for me through it all. He was my backbone and my best friend. *Look at me, getting all teary-eyed like an ex-husband in divorce court.*

My moment was interrupted by the ringing of my BlackBerry cell phone.

"This is Karen."

"Hi Karen, this is Tyson."

"Hey, Tyson."

"I was calling to see if you found the data that we needed on the Weber account."

"Actually, I did. It's funny that you called. I just recently completed a spreadsheet that breaks down all of the details for us."

"That's great. Is it alright if I stop by your desk so that we can go over it together?"

"Only if you bring me a cup of coffee."

"I am on my way."

Tyson arrived at my desk ten minutes after our phone conversation—with a cup of coffee in his hand. Tyson placed the cup of coffee on my desk, and then he placed two packets of sugar next to it. I thanked him for the coffee as I tore open the sugar packets and poured their contents into my coffee. I grabbed a plastic spoon out of my center desk drawer, and I stirred my coffee until all of the sugar dissolved. Tyson watched as I took my first sip of the recently delivered, fresh coffee. As I sipped my coffee, the vitalizing aroma rushed into my nostrils and invigorated my brain. I smiled to illustrate my endorsement.

Tyson positioned a chair on my side of the desk, and he sat down next to me. Every movement that he made left an airborne trace of his signature scent. I opened the Excel file that I had created and showed Tyson the information that I had collected. We both looked over the data. In the middle of our assessment of the information displayed in front of us, Tyson's attention was diverted to the pictures located above my computer monitor.

"That's a nice picture of you."

"Thank you."

"Is that your boyfriend in the picture with you?"

"Fiancé."

"Oh, well, excuse me."

Tyson laughed as he raised his eyebrows and placed both of his hands into the air in a teasing manner. His sarcastic gesture made me laugh with him. I tried to continue with our work, but Tyson kept asking me questions about Tony.

"How long have you been engaged?"

"We've been engaged for a few months."

"Congratulations."

"Thank you."

"So, when is the wedding?"

"We haven't set a date for it yet."

"What colors did you select for the wedding?"

"I haven't done all of that yet."

"Well, it doesn't seem like you have done much of anything for the wedding so far."

"If you would spend as much time on this account as you are spending enquiring about my business, then we would get a lot of work accomplished."

"Ouch. I didn't mean to be nosy. I was just making conversation."

"No, you weren't. You were being nosy."

"Okay. Maybe you are right."

We both laughed as Tyson tried to disguise the embarrassing look he had on his face.

10 Tyson

I had the whole loft smelling like Burberry cologne. The lights were dimmed, and Kem was playing in the background. You couldn't tell me that I didn't know how to set the mood. I even ordered some food from Ruth's Chris over on Illinois Street and picked it up on my way home from work. I gently placed the well-done steaks on my dishes and strategically lined up the sides next to the steaks to make it look as if I had slaved over the stove and made the meal myself.

I was clean. My scalp was freshly shaven, and my face was tapered perfectly, thanks to the barber shop on the corner of 38th and Lafayette Road. My cologne matched the room's aroma, and my shoes matched my belt. I had on so much gator that you would think I had a hunting license. I had on dark brown slacks and a dark brown button-up to match. The top two buttons on my shirt were left open. If you haven't figured it out by now, I had a lady visitor on her way to my love den.

I met Joan at Black Expo about a month ago. She interviewed me on the street for her media class at IUPUI. She was a twenty-two-year-old journalism student at the university. Now, this girl was fine. She had cappuccino-colored skin that was smooth and radiant. Her hair was short and natural. Most women would not be able to pull off the natural hair thing, but this girl had it perfected. Her eyes were bright and slightly slanted. She had a cute little button nose and a sexy wide mouth. As she interviewed me, I could not help but to stare at the medium-brown lipstick she was wearing. Every word that her lips formed had me anticipating the next vowel. Baby girl had it going on. After the interview, we had a twenty-minute conversation, and then she gave me her number. I called her maybe once or twice before I asked her over to my place that night.

At about seven, my house phone rang. It was Joan. She was downstairs and was ready to come up to the loft. I buzzed her in, and I walked into the hallway of my building so that I could greet her at the elevator. As soon as the elevator door opened, Joan stepped out. *Oh, my God!* She looked even better tonight than she did that day on the street. Joan had on a black, sleeveless, twist-front dress that draped just below her knees. She also had on large, white-gold hoop earrings, and her makeup was faultless. To top

60

it all off, she was wearing black, peep-toe pumps that showed off her skillfully manicured toes. I readied my deep voice.

"Hey. You look beautiful."

Joan smiled and formed her lips to respond. "Well, thank you. You are looking rather handsome yourself."

We hugged and I gave her a soft kiss on her right cheek. She smelled very good.

"Did you have a hard time finding my building?"

"No, not at all. It was actually very easy with the directions you gave me."

I walked her into my loft, and I received an instant response for all the trouble I had gone through in preparation for this date. Joan was wearing a smile that extended from one ear to the other. She complimented me on the way my loft was decorated. She also thanked me for having things arranged so nicely for our date.

"You even cooked for me? Oh, my God. I think that you are the first man to ever do that for me. You definitely get extra brownie points for that. I really love the way it looks and smells in here. I can't believe you did all of this for me."

That is the exact reaction I was looking for. I was definitely in good standing. We could have probably skipped dinner and drinks and headed straight to the bedroom if I had wanted to, but I wouldn't let that happen. I paid a lot for that steak dinner, and I would be damned if I didn't get to enjoy it. I placed my hand on the small of her back, and I guided her across the dark brown hardwood floors to my mahogany wood dining room table. I pulled her chair back, and she eased into her seat.

We talked a lot during dinner. Joan told me about the many plays she had been in at the university. She also explained how thrilled she was about an upcoming play that she was going to be in. I just let her go on. She talked and talked. I didn't even care about anything that she was saying. As she talked, I just stared into those slanted eyes. As long as she was staring back, whatever she was saying was alright with me. Hell, she could have said something bad about my mama or something. It would not have mattered. Or, maybe I might not have heard it because I really wasn't listening.

After dinner, I poured red wine into two glasses, and we sat in the living room and continued our date. Joan began to tell me about the different roles that she'd had in the many plays she'd been in. She told me about how she had to act out crying scenes as well as kissing scenes. I felt that this was the time that I should start working my game. I had listened to her talk about herself for about an hour. The entire time, I was just listening and waiting for an intro. This was what I was waiting for.

"So, when you do your kissing scenes, do you actually kiss the other actors?"

"Not really. We just touch lips. No tongue involved."

I gave her an innocent smile. "Well, if it were me, I would be content with that. Just having my lips touch yours would be sufficient for me. I don't see how the actors do it."

She smiled and started to blush a little. "Awe, you are so charming. I have an idea. How would you like to do a scene with me right now?"

"How would we do that? Did you bring a script with you or something?"

"No, silly. We don't need a script. We can just make it up as we go."

I sat up straight on the couch. Now this was my kind of date. Maybe we could do a scene from a porno or something. I had seen so many of them that I could probably recite a few lines with her.

"Alright," I said. "Since you are the professional, you start it off. Now remember, I am an amateur at this. So, take it easy on me."

She showed me her smile and started to get into character. She grabbed my right hand and held it between both of hers. She kissed it and began to act.

"Tyson, you have been gone for so long. I have been going crazy without you. While you were away fighting for our country, I was here waiting anxiously for your return."

I tried to hold back the giggles. I wanted to laugh so hard, but I didn't.

"Joan, I was thinking of you every minute that I was away. In fact, it was my love for you that kept me alive. I fought and I fought, knowing that you would be here waiting for my return."

I was really putting some skills into my part. I looked her in her eyes and made a caring face and everything.

"Tell me. Tell me, Tyson. What is it about me that you missed the most? What was it that kept you alive for me?"

"It was everything. I missed your eyes and your cute little nose. I missed the way that you would call my name when we made love. I missed holding you in my arms in the morning. Most of all, I missed your kisses. Your kisses were the blood that pumped through my veins while I was away."

Now, I don't know if it was because my acting was great or if she was planning to do it the whole time, but as soon as I said that, she kissed me. This was not an acting kiss either. There was lots of tongue in this one. As a matter of fact, it involved a very soft tongue, one that danced with my tongue as if it were exploring it. Up and down, and even in circles. We kissed for a long time. As the time passed, the kisses developed more passion. Joan was a great kisser. Her wide mouth almost swallowed my lips whole. She was a very passionate kisser. I mean, this girl knew how to kiss. She would pull her lips away from mine after gently inserting her tongue in my mouth. It was like she was teasing me. Before she would re-insert her tongue, she would gently suck on my top lip. After that, she would suck on my bottom lip. The whole time, we were both breathing heavily.

After a while, she climbed on top of me. I was sitting upright, and she was straddling me. Joan looked down at me from her superior position and began to unbutton my shirt. The whole time she was staring at me with those gorgeous eyes and biting her bottom lip in a naughty sort of gesture. Joan gently drew imaginary designs on my bare chest with her index finger. It was almost as if she was marking her territory. She then helped me out of my shirt and began to kiss my neck. She slowly eased from my neck down to my shoulders. While she was kissing my shoulders, she was caressing my biceps with both of her hands. I was really feeling it. The entire time I was in awe. I had this natural goddess on top of me, seducing me like I was her dream guy. The whole time I was harder than a table leg.

After Joan excited me for about ten minutes, she got off me and stood right in front of me. She kicked off her peep-toe black heels and pushed them to the side with her left foot. Joan then started to ease her dress down her body. Slowly, inch by inch, her body was exposed to me. As her dress fell beneath her cleavage, inside I was excited like a kid on Christmas morning. Her breasts were beautiful. Her perky C-cups were decorated with nickel-sized, brown nipples. After her dress passed her breasts, I was then enticed with the view of her stomach. It was flat, with a single, vertical indenture, which ran from her ribs down to her navel. It was evident that she worked out a lot. Her stomach was muscular, but feminine. Her hips were striking. Joan had curves in all the right places. As her dress passed below her hips, she allowed it to fall to the ground. By this time, I was really ready to do some damage. She grabbed my hand and made me stand up in front of her. She placed one of my hands on her breast and the other on her waist.

"So, does this beautiful loft have a nice bed-room?"

She had a look on her face like she had some more acting techniques to show me. I tried to sound like I was still cool and in control.

"It sure does. Would you like to see it?"

"Don't mind if I do."

After that brief moment of dialog, I led her up the iron stairway to the bedroom of my loft.

11 Tyson

As soon as we made it to my bedroom that overlooked the downstairs of my loft, Joan eased onto my bed. She was lying on her back and was propped up on both of her elbows. One of her feet barely touched the bedroom's hardwood floor. Her opposite knee was bent toward the ceiling, and her toes straddled the edge of the bed. The city lights that crept through my bedroom window and her silhouette looked really good on my expensive comforter set. I was ready to give a new meaning to Linens 'n Things. I hurried out of my pants and boxers like I was going to lose this moment if I didn't. I was butt-naked with church-socks on. I walked over to my naked lady and comforter set as cool as I could. I stretched out both of my hands to pull her black-laced thong from around her waist. As I did that, she arched her back in one sexy motion. As I maneuvered her thong past her feet, she slowly spread her legs open. Joan did not say a word, but her actions were telling me that she was open for business. I eased my body on top of hers.

68

The sexual tension in the room was thick. I kissed her wide mouth and she smiled. I kissed her slim neck and she squirmed. I kissed her left breast and she moaned. I did not want to discriminate, so I made sure that I gave her right breast just as much attention as I did the left. I wet my tongue and made a trail from the center of her cleavage down to her belly button. After that, I gently blew on the saliva road that I had just created. Joan's back arched, and she grabbed her natural hair with both of her hands. I then allowed my tongue to make a ten-inch leap over her vagina, and it landed on her right inner thigh. I sucked on her skin seductively, but not hard enough to leave a mark. I was so close to her neatly trimmed private that I could smell her clean aroma. It was like waking up in the morning to the smell of fresh coffee brewing. I could not help but to smile in approval. My lips and tongue worked their way down to her knees. My tongue made circular journeys around her knee cap. Then I raised her leg and gave her calf some attention. Her legs were muscular, but feminine.

By this time, she was ready to explode like a suicide bomber. I lowered her leg and crawled across the bed over to my nightstand. I opened the single drawer and grabbed a condom. I had lots of different kinds of condoms, but this time I happened to grab a Trojan condom with the light-blue wrapping. I then sat on the edge of my bed, and I tore a corner of the light-blue wrapper open with my teeth. I then released the condom from its confinement and unrolled the Trojan onto my love stick. I was now armed and ready for sexual combat with my naked journalism major from IUPUI.

As I eased back on top of Joan, she raised her head off my comforter to kiss me. I met her halfway. We kissed with more passion than we had done before. As we kissed, I slowly entered her love canal. At that moment, she wrapped both of her legs around my waist and arched her back. She stopped kissing me and placed the side of her face against mine. Her left hand palmed my right shoulder blade while her right hand caressed my scalp. The sound of horns blaring from the traffic outside my window was in my left ear, and her sensual moans were in my right ear. After about five minutes of doing it her way, I parted my face from hers and rested on my hands. My slow and short thrusts became fast and deep. Joan adjusted to my change of pace. She placed one hand on my chest, and the other was on the small of my back. She pushed my chest as I went in, and she pulled my waist toward her as I pulled away. Her moans increased in volume. Our bodies were in rhythm. She lifted her butt off the bed and began to thrust me back. We were both really into it at this point. Sweat dripped from my forehead to her cheek.

Joan looked at me with half-opened eyes and told me to roll over onto my back. Her voice was airy and soft like she was out of breath. I obeyed her request. She climbed on top of me and fit our pieces back in place. Her knees were on either side of me. Both of her hands were on my chest, and her head was tilted back. Her breasts hung over me like imported African chandeliers. Her stomach was covered with a mist of sweat. Joan's motions were mathematical. She was rotating her hips in a 360-degree radius. She then looked me in my face.

"Do you like it?"

"Yes."

"Tell me you like it."

"I like it."

Joan's body then began to jerk like she had stuck a paper clip into an electrical outlet while she was standing in a puddle of water. Her moans then reached a higher pitch. She continued to thrust in spite of her orgasm. This time more aggressively than before. A feeling came over me. My breath became shallow, my face caught chills, and my body tensed up like I was waiting for an explosion. Then it happened. I began to jolt like I was having a seizure. I lost all ability to speak, and drool ran from the corner of my mouth down the side of my cheek. Joan collapsed on me. The kids that weren't going to make it filled the condom. I fell asleep.

12 Tony

I hadn't been able to get Laura out of my mind since last night. It had been so long since the last time I had seen her that I almost forgot how I felt about her. I started to remember all of the things that I liked about her. All of the things that made me fall in love with her in the first place started to haunt me. I almost forgot about her smile that had the ability to reverse a bad day. I even forgot about those eyes that could burn a love hole into your soul. My mind was running all night. I could not get any sleep. Every time that I would fall asleep, I would have a dream about Laura. Laura was on my mind all night.

I really wanted to pick up my cell phone and call her. Of course, that would probably be a bad idea with my fiancée sleeping right next to me. Every time that I woke up from one of my Laura dreams, I was scared that I might have called her name during my sleep.

During my many dreams of Laura during the night, I almost forgot one important issue. She left me. She moved away from me. Just gave up on me and moved away. I had all of these plans for the both of us and our future together. I had it all planned out. I knew what type of cars we were going to drive, the kind of house that I wanted us to live in, and even the day care that we would send our kids to. All of this was for nothing. All of this planning, just so she could walk out on me. When we talked on the phone after she left, she explained to me the reason why she left me. Laura said that she was waiting on the day that I would make her my wife, but it never came. All of our friends were getting engaged, and I hadn't popped the question to her yet.

I told her that I was planning on asking her to marry me one day, but she wasn't going for it. She thought I was just saying that to get her back. Laura said I was just telling her what she wanted to hear. I really *was* planning on marrying her. I just didn't know when that was going to be. Something was holding up the progress. I think the fact that I was afraid was the main reason. I was in my early twenties. I didn't have a high-paying job, and I didn't know the first thing about taking care of a family. I could barely take care of myself. I just didn't think it would have been fair for me to bring someone else into my debts and struggles. It was this way of thinking that caused me to lose my girl.

74

After last night, I was totally out of it all day at work. I was working on only a couple hours of sleep. I just kept looking at the napkin that Laura had written her number on. Part of me wanted to just dial the number to see what would happen. The other part wanted to throw the napkin into the trash and call my fiancée. My mind was racing all day. Was Laura really my soul mate? Did I try hard enough to get her back when she left, or did I let my ego take over? Why didn't I just move to Texas to be with her? What would have happened if I would have kept in contact with her? Am I really in love with Karen? Do I love Karen more than I loved Laura? Is Karen my soul mate? Do I still love Laura? Is it possible to be in love with two women at the same time? So many questions, but not enough answers.

I talked to a lot of people who came up to the car lot. Everyone was "just looking" today. We just got the new 3-Series BMW in this morning, and it was creating quite a buzz. The entire time that I was carrying on conversations, trying to get a sale, that napkin was burning a hole in my back pocket. I tried to keep myself busy so that I would not have to face the many questions that were floating around in my head. Jay had the day off today, so at least I didn't have to hear him give me a hard time, although he did keep sending me text messages. Each message was telling me not to call Laura. Jay knew the whole story about Laura and me and how things went down. He always said that we broke up for a reason and, if we didn't break up, then I would not have gotten engaged to Karen. Jay always told me how good a woman Karen is. Even though he gave me a lot of crap about my being whipped and all, he really did like and respect Karen.

Toward the end of my busy day, my conscience was starting to get the best of me. I started to feel guilty about even accepting Laura's number. How would I feel if Karen accepted a phone number from one of her old boyfriends? I would be really hurt if I ever heard about it. Karen trusted me, and I was putting her trust to test by contemplating calling my ex. Not only was she my ex, but she was the woman whom I considered my soul mate. At this point, I felt as if everyone at the car lot knew what I was up to. I felt like that small napkin with Laura's number on it had grown to the size of a phone book. Everyone looked at me with pity in their eyes. They knew what I was thinking. They knew about my ex-girlfriend that I wanted to call. They knew about my beautiful, innocent fiancée who trusted me so. I could see people whispering about me. They were pointing at the phone book that was erupting out the back pocket of my khakis. I was really starting to lose my mind.

Then, my cell phone rang and almost scared me into a heart attack. It was Karen. I cleared my throat.

"Hello?"

"Hey baby, what's up?"

"Nothing much, just trying to sell some cars and make that money. What's up with you?"

"Nothing. Working my butt off."

"Well, that is a lot of work, because you sure got a lot of butt."

We both started to laugh.

"You are so silly. I was calling you to let you know that I am going to be working a little late tonight. My team and I are behind on some things, and we are going to stay and try to get caught up."

I tried to hide my disappointment. I had actually been looking forward to seeing Karen after work. I wanted to spend time with her to keep my mind off Laura. She had been working so much lately that we didn't get to spend a lot of time together.

"No problem, babe. I guess that I will see you whenever you get home."

"Alright, I love you, and I will see you tonight."

"Love you, too."

"Bye."

"Bye."

I inhaled deep and let out a long exhale as my eyes scaled the BMW parking lot. Disappointment filled my face. This late-night working stuff was becoming an everyday event for Karen. I understood that she was doing what she had to do in order to get to where she wanted to be with her career. I also understood that this behavior was expected when you were connected to a corporate woman. I had no problems with that. But I did have a problem with her neglecting me in the process. It had been weeks since the last time we went out together. When she came home from her long days, she fell asleep on the sofa before we could even spend an ounce of quality time together.

The worst part was, when she did get home from work at a reasonable time, she spent hours working on her laptop and talking to coworkers on her cell phone. The whole time I'd just sit there, watching television as if I were alone in our apartment. Her work never ended. It was leaving for work by seven in the morning, lunch meetings with coworkers, coming home after seven at night, jumping on her laptop as soon as she got home, having a couple of work-related conversations on her cell, and then falling asleep on the sofa, fully dressed with her laptop in standby mode. I didn't even get to talk to her during the day anymore. Whenever I called her on my breaks at work, she was always in some kind of meeting. How many meetings do you need in order to get the job done?

We used to talk all the time during our days. I always called her whenever I could get away from customers at the car lot. Even if it was just for a few minutes, I liked to call her to see how her day was going. Karen would do the same on her end, too. Now, all of that had changed. This new position had become the other man.

13 Karen

The tension in the conference room was thick. My manager was adamant on sticking to the original time line that was given to us on this project. The way that he kept rubbing his hand on his scalp made it clear as to why he only had hair on the sides and the back of his head. With every rub, his bald spot appeared to be getting shinier. He continued to pace in front of the dry erase board that was on the wall on the south side of the conference room. It was covered with a schedule and a flowchart that was related to our project. It looked as if both had been drawn by a three-year-old with a nervous condition.

My manager was dressed in a wrinkled, blue dress shirt and navy blue slacks. His yellow and red striped tie was loose around his neck, and the top button of his wrinkled shirt was open. He had both of his sleeves rolled up to his forearms, and he was sweating profusely. Tyson and my manager were going back and forth about where we were with the progress of our project. Tyson calmly backed his arguments and handled the battle as smooth as it could be handled. He produced records of the update meetings that we'd had with the execs from Weber Grille. He was also able to show records of the creative meetings we'd had as a team. Tyson assured my manager that the Weber Grille execs were fully aware of everything that was taking place with the project and that they were in full support of it.

As Tyson spoke, he used his hands to help form his words. His argument was articulate, and he didn't raise his voice above normal conversation level. If you were new to the company and you just happened to walk into the room, you would think that Tyson was the manager. As he spoke, he would on occasion look to me for confirmation on his argued points. I was sitting next to Tyson at the conference table, so I would pass Tyson information as he needed it. I also helped out a lot in our meeting. I showed my manager the different ideas and designs that we had been working on. I was able to show him one of the favored graphics that I had created for a possible website advertisement. Tyson and I were doing all of the talking while the rest of our team just sat there in silence. It was easy to see who the all-stars of this team were.

After about an hour and a half of successfully supporting our current progress on the new account, the meeting was over. I just sat in my leather chair and collected my thoughts as everyone hurried out of the room. My eyes were closed, and I was massaging my temples with both of my index fingers. I was just trying to steal a few minutes of sanity. My throat was dry, and my brown-leather Nine West heels were hurting my feet.

"You alright?" Tyson asked.

His voice startled me. I didn't know that he was standing next to me. I thought I was the only one left in the conference room. I straightened my posture and crossed my legs.

"Yes, I'm fine. Just trying to let it all soak in."

"I know. It has been a long morning, huh?"

"Long and grueling. There is just so much to do and not enough time to do it."

"Well, that's the wonderful world that we work in. This place will drive you crazy if you let it. Accounts are always too big, and the time lines are always small."

"Amen to that."

I found a smile as I said that. I stood up and adjusted the collar to my beige blouse. Tyson pulled the chair out of my way so that I could step away from the conference table. He stopped me as I started to exit the room.

"Hey. Do you want to go and get some lunch before it gets too late? You know how quickly things around here can get hectic. If we don't go now, then we might not get a lunch."

"Sure. That's a great idea. That way we can get energized to complete the day. I didn't get a chance to eat any breakfast this morning, so I am starved."

"Great. Does Rockbottom sound good to you?"

"Sounds great."

"Well, Rockbottom it is."

We walked through the aisles of our fourth-floor office as fast as we could so that we would not be noticed. We did not want to be sucked into a serious conversation with a manager or coworker about time lines and creative thinking. The entire time that we were walking through the stress-filled environment that we call work, noise was all around us. I heard the sound of cell phones ringing, people being paged over the intercom system, employees having heated discussions, and the sound of fingertips tapping computer keyboards, all culminating to form a very annoying sound track.

As we exited the suite that houses our offices and entered the fourth-floor hallway, we both let out long exhales. Tyson looked at me, and I knew that we were on the same page. We were both glad that we had made it out of there with our sanity intact. I slung my oversized brown and khaki Coach purse over my shoulder and headed for the elevators. Tyson was walking beside me. When we arrived at the elevators and we stopped moving, Tyson reached out to press the down arrow for the elevators. As he reached for the button, the sleeve to his blue suit jacket pulled back a little. I noticed that he had on a tailored, light blue shirt with platinum cuff links. He was also wearing a silver-colored Movado watch.

Tyson was clearly a man with a lot of style. I had never seen him at work looking less than perfect. His head was always clean shaven, and his face neatly trimmed. His clothes always looked clean and crisp. If I did not know any better, I would think that he had his very own drycleaners and barber shop located in his home. Whenever Tyson walked into a room, a fresh cologne scent rushed in right behind him. If anyone was paying attention, they would see all the ladies in the room close their eyes, take deep breaths, and enjoy the aroma.

"Nice purse."

As Tyson spoke, I could smell the fresh scent of Altoids on his breath mixed with the aroma of his signature aftershave.

"Thanks."

I smiled without showing teeth and raised my eyebrows. I knew that he was just trying to be nice and spark some kind of conversation, but Tyson's personality was sometimes flirty. The way that he talked to you could get you into trouble. It's not like he was rude or anything, but Tyson talked to women like women liked to be talked to. It's kind of like when you talk to a baby in that baby-talk voice. That just makes a baby's day. That baby's face will light up, and the baby will smile and show you a mouth full of gums. Well, I guess it's the same with women. Tyson talked to women in a calm, deep, low voice. He always smiled when he talked and stared directly into your eyes. He maintained eye contact with you the entire conversation, which gives a woman the impression that nothing else in the room matters except for her. His eyes gave you his full, undivided attention. And believe me, we women love attention.

We decided to walk to Rockbottom since it was only a few blocks from the firm. The sun was shining, and a slight breeze cruised around the downtown Indianapolis buildings. The sidewalk traffic was busy because of the time of the day. It felt good to be out of the office for a change. I tried to capture the images and the smells of outside. As we passed the corner of Washington and Illinois, a man was playing his saxophone for tips. He was dressed as if he was homeless, and his hair was nappy and long. Some people were standing there listening to him play, and others were walking by. A man dropped a couple of singles into the hat that the musician had upside down on the ground in front of him.

He was actually good at playing that sax. The melodies he produced permeated the downtown air. As he played, his eyes were closed, and he appeared to be smiling. I wondered what it was that he may have been thinking about. I wondered if that saxophone was his only sanity in a world of insanity. Tyson dropped a five into the hat and lightly patted the man's shoulder as we walked by. It was almost as if Tyson was letting the man know that everything was going to be alright.

"So, you do have a heart underneath all of those degrees and promotions, huh?" I said to him.

"Of course I do. Sometimes it takes a scene like that for us to realize how blessed we are to live the type of lives that we live. It makes whatever drama that is around you, no matter how big, seem small. It could always be worse."

That thought remained with me. Tyson was right. It could always be worse. I had been so stressed lately. I had been stressed with my job and my relationship. There were just not enough hours in the day. I worked hard all day, and I tried to keep on track with at least fifty percent of my schedule. Then, I came home to a neglected fiancé. But it didn't end there. After I got home to Tony, my phone continued to ring, and the e-mails just kept coming. I was glad that I had a man like Tony by my side. He really understood what it was that I was trying to do. He really supported my dreams and aspirations. I knew that it would all be worth it in the end, and Tony did also.

We arrived at Rockbottom after our fifteen-minute, sun-filled walk from the fourth-floor slave ship. It was packed with the lunch crowd. The chatter of loud conversations filled the restaurant. A young Asian girl with medium-length, jet-black hair greeted us as we walked through the entrance of the restaurant. Shortly after she asked us how many would be joining us for lunch, another young girl with long, blonde hair and green eyes showed us to our booth. She told us her name and asked us if we knew what we wanted to drink. Tyson told her that he already knew what he wanted to eat and to drink and asked me if I was ready to order. It was obvious that Tyson was trying to get our orders in early so that they could get started on cooking our meals. I nodded my head to let him know that I was ready also.

"I will have the macaroni bowl and a water with lemon," I told her.

The waitress cued Tyson that it was his turn to order.

"And I'll have the barbecue pizza with a strawberry lemonade to drink."

As we waited for our food to arrive, Tyson looked into my eyes and began to speak.

"So, Ms. Karen, what is it that you like to do whenever you get any time to do it?"

"Excuse me?"

"Hobbies. You know, things that you like to do in your spare time. Judging from your appearance, I can tell that you get a good workout at least twice a week. I can also tell that you get your hair done weekly. But other than working out and sitting in a beauty shop all day, what else do you like to do?"

"For your information, Mr. Tyson, I work out at least three times a week. I would like to work out more, but I can't seem to find the time. Usually, if I do manage to find some time away from work, I try to spend as much of it as I can with my fiancé."

"Oh, yeah. The fiancé. I almost forgot that you were engaged."

"I'm sure that you did, or at least you would like to."

"Wow. Low blow. I was just saying that we are both running around like chickens with their heads cut off so much at the office that I forgot."

88

"I'm sorry. I am just a little on edge. Maybe I'll feel a little nicer after I get something to eat. I haven't eaten all day, and my stomach is growling louder than a pit bull."

After our food arrived at our table, Tyson and I talked the entire time we were at Rockbottom. Neither one of us talked about anything that had to do with work. We just got to know each other. He was actually a really cool guy. We talked and laughed as we ate. Tyson had a dry sense of humor and cute dimples. Every time that he laughed, his dimples would appear and steal the show. I talked about Tony and how long we had been dating. Tyson told me about some of the girls that he was dating. He was very upfront about his dating life. He was very honest in talking about the types of women he had dated in the past. Any fool could see that he had a way with women. I could see how one could fall for him. Tyson was very attractive, had a great career, and had a down-to-earth personality.

As we were finishing up our meal, Tyson's BlackBerry phone rang. He answered it after a couple of rings and began to speak. You could see the frustration in his face. His whole attitude changed. Tyson sat up straight in the booth and adjusted his tie. Soon after, he ended the call.

"That was the office. They are looking for us. Evidently there are lots of things that need to be done, and no one knows how to do it except for us."

"Well, I guess that is our cue."

"Yes, it is."

I grabbed my purse, Tyson took care of the check, I left the tip, and we headed out of the restaurant. The sun seemed to be a little brighter than it was when we were on our way to the restaurant. I reached inside my purse and grabbed my shades.

"Go ahead, Hollywood!" Tyson was laughing and shaking his head.

"Whatever. Don't be mad just because you don't have a pair of your own."

At that very moment, Tyson reached inside his suit jacket and pulled out a case. He opened it and pulled out a very nice pair of Gucci sunglasses. As he placed them onto his square face, he looked at me with those bedroom eyes and replied, "Who doesn't have a pair?"

We both began to laugh. This guy was so cocky. His personal confidence was at a level that I had never witnessed in another individual before. We joked and talked a little more before we arrived at the front doors of our office building. We both took in deep breaths, and Tyson reached for the door.

14 Tony

I got home from the car lot a little before seven o' clock in the evening. The west-side apartment that Karen and I shared was dark. It was obvious that no one had been there since this morning when Karen and I both left for work. I turned on the lamp in the living room and placed my keys on the table next to the door. My eyes took in the emptiness of the room, and I took in a deep breath. The only noise throughout the entire apartment was the sound coming from the DVR that was recording the last of the six o' clock news. Karen always set the timer for the DVR to record the news because she never knew how late she was going to work.

I walked into the kitchen and opened the white, side-by-side refrigerator. I glanced at the three empty shelves. At that moment, I noticed that Karen hadn't been to Kroger to pick up any groceries. I opened the freezer side of the refrigerator and was introduced to equal disappointment. I wasn't that hungry when I first walked into the apartment, but as soon as I saw that we needed groceries, my stomach started making more noises than a backseat on prom night. I was starving. I opened a couple of cabinets and began to get a little frustrated. It was at that moment that I opened my cell phone and looked up the number to Pizza Hut, which was programmed into my contacts. I ordered a large pizza with hamburger meat and Italian sausage. Before I ended the call, the girl on the phone told me that it would be forty-five minutes before my pizza would be delivered.

I called Karen on her cell phone. It rang three times, and then it went to voicemail. I didn't leave a message. I placed my cell phone on the coffee table and just sat there for a moment. I was really irritated. Karen was working late, there was no food in the apartment, and I had to order a pizza for dinner. The least that she could do was answer her phone. I let ten minutes pass before I tried to call her again. She finally answered.

"Hello?"

"What's up?"

"Nothing, just working. What's up with you, babe?"

"I just got home not too long ago. I had to order a pizza for dinner. I ordered a large just in case you're hungry when you get home from work."

"Oh, I should be alright. Tyson and I ate at Rockbottom for lunch earlier, and I've been snacking on Trail Mix all evening."

"Well, it will be here if you do get hungry. Anyway, how is the rest of your day going?"

"Very busy. I have been working nonstop. I have had two meetings since the last time that I talked to you today. On top of that, it looks like I will be here for about another hour or so, and then I'll still have some things to take care of when I get home. What about you? How was your day?"

"It was kind of stressful. I was tired all day long and—"

Before I could finish my statement, Karen began to talk to someone in the background as if she hadn't been in the middle of a conversation with me. I was trying to tell her about my day, and she just ignored me and began a conversation with another person in the room. I waited.

"I'm sorry, baby. Tyson was asking me about the presentation we have to do tomorrow. Can I call you from the car when I'm leaving the office?"

"Sure. No problem."

"Alright, I'll talk to you then. Bye."

"Bye."

It was as if my day hadn't even mattered to her. I was considerate enough to ask her about her day and listen to her complain about how busy it was. But when it came time for me to talk about my day, it didn't matter. It just wasn't important to her. I understood that Karen was trying to take her career to the next level, and I was in support of that all the way. But was it worth losing each other in the process? We barely even saw each other anymore, and we lived underneath the same roof. I hardly even got to talk to her on the phone during the day anymore. Maybe I should've said something to her about it. But I didn't want her to think that I didn't support her. I certainly didn't want to add to her stress.

I picked up my cell and called Jay. He answered after the phone rang a couple of times.

"Hello?"

"What's up, man? It's Tony."

"Nothing much. What's up with you, bro?"

"Same crap, different day."

"I hear you."

"I just ordered some pizza, and it should be here in a few. You are welcome to have some if you want."

"The old lady is working late again, huh?"

"Ding, ding, ding. You have just guessed the million-dollar answer."

I couldn't disguise my sarcasm. I usually didn't like to bring other people into my business, but I was feeling really frustrated.

"That's cool, bro. I will be there in about fifteen minutes. Do you want me to pick us up some drinks on my way over?"

"Yes, sir. Make mine a Sprite."

"Will do. I will be there in a few."

After I ended my call with Jay, I walked over to the computer hutch, which was located on a wall between our living room and dining room. I opened the double-doors and pulled the keyboard drawer toward me. I then grabbed a chair from the dining room and sat in front of the computer to check my e-mail. Ten minutes later, the pizza guy arrived, and ten minutes after that, Jay arrived. When Jay got there, we demolished the entire pizza in less than fifteen minutes. When we were done, the pizza box looked like a victim in a murder scene. There were pizza sauce fingerprints everywhere. Only a few sausages were left behind at the scene of the crime.

We were stuffed. Jay and I watched ESPN as we joked and talked. After about an hour of hanging out, Jay headed back home.

15 Tyson

My team and I were at the office until about ten o' clock in the evening. Everyone was beginning to show signs of fatigue, so we decided to call it a night. This turned out to be a very long day for me. I came into work at about eight o' clock and worked hard the entire time. Karen and I got a lot of work completed during the process of our long day. She had really surprised me. I did not know that she was this good at what she does. Karen was a very determined individual. She liked to get things done right the first time. Karen was results driven and paid lots of attention to detail. It would be very hard for a mistake to slip through the cracks on her watch.

Karen was parked in the parking garage over on Meridian Street. I was able to park in the lot right next to our office building, so I offered to drive her to her car. I carried her laptop bag for her as we walked to my car. We were both obviously exhausted. I opened the passenger-side door to my car, and I waited until she was situated before I closed it. I walked around to my side of the car and got in. I started the engine and turned up the air conditioner.

"Wow. That feels really good."

Karen pulled her hair back from her face and let the air hit her. She then closed her eyes and smiled softly. She looked beautiful. Her hair was black and straight. Her complexion was clear and smooth.

"I see that I'm not the only one who is happy to get out of there."

I loosened my tie and placed the car in reverse. As we drove the short distance to the garage where Karen's car was, we talked about how long our day had been. We both laughed at how useless the rest of our team was. Karen and I were the stars of the team, and we both knew it. Karen pointed at a building to our right.

"There is the garage right there."

I pulled the car over and turned on my hazards. I then hopped out of the car and rushed to her side to open the door for her. Karen got out of the car and did an inventory check to make sure that she was not leaving anything behind. I held the door as she moved out of the way, and then I closed it.

"Do you need me to walk you to your car?"

"No. I should be fine. But thank you for the ride. That was very nice of you."

"No problem. I can't have you out here walking to the garage late at night by yourself. Why aren't you parking in the company lot next to the office?"

"That lot has a limited number of spaces. Only the hotshots like yourself are privileged enough to have assigned spaces in that lot. The other free spaces fill up really quickly."

"Oh. So they didn't give you an assigned spot?"

"Nope. Not yet."

"Wait right here."

I walked over to the driver's side and opened the door. I grabbed my parking permit that was hanging from the rear-view mirror. I walked back around the car to where Karen was standing.

"Here is a present from the hotshot. You can have my parking space." I handed her the parking permit.

"I can't take your parking space from you. You earned that spot."

"I insist. I get here earlier than you do anyway. I would have a better chance at getting into one of those free spots than you do. This way, you won't have to worry about going into that garage late at night."

Karen smiled and took the permit from me. Her eyes showed me how thankful she was. She then gave me a hug.

"That is so nice of you. I really appreciate it."

After that, Karen smiled at me again, and then she turned around and started to walk toward the entrance of the parking garage. She looked back at me once more before she closed the glass door behind her. I watched her walk into the building and continued to watch her until I couldn't see her anymore. I then jumped into my car and drove off.

On the way home, I called Joan to see if she wanted to come over. Joan accepted and told me that she would be over to my place in about an hour. She said that she was nearing the completion of some homework, which worked out perfect for me. It gave me enough time to make it home and unwind a little. After I ended the call with Joan, I drove the rest of the way home in complete silence. All that could be heard were the sounds of the road. My mind was racing with all kinds of thoughts: everything from work, to Joan, and even Karen entered my thoughts.

Joan was a sweet girl. She had a bright future ahead of her. Whenever she graduated from IUPUI, she wouldn't have a hard time at all finding a job. Joan had everything you could ask for in a woman. She was naturally beautiful, and her body was breathtaking. She was very intelligent and treated me well. I could call her with a need in the middle of the night, and she would make sure that I was taken care of. And the sex. Oh, the sex. The sex was awesome. I'd had sex with my share of women, but sex with Joan was on another level. I had never experienced passion before I met Joan. Our encounters were passionate. I really liked the way that she reacted while we were having sex. She made me feel like I was the best lover in the world. Everything, from the faces that she made to the moans that she screamed out, really fed my sex ego.

On the other hand, there was something about Karen that really sparked my interest. She was a classy chick. To see her in business attire and high heels was a sight to behold. Her hair was always flowing, and she had a smile that could light up any room. I knew that she was engaged, but obviously the brother was not doing what he should. I could still recall how she looked back at me before she closed the door to the parking garage. It was a look of curiosity. It was as if she was wondering what it would be like to get involved with me. Besides, a happily engaged woman would not have hugged me the way that she did. When she hugged me, she really clinched me tight. I could feel her hands grabbing my back as she rested her head on my shoulder. That was not your typical friendly hug. That hug meant something.

16 Tony

Karen got home a little after eleven. I was in bed by then, but I wasn't asleep. I was watching re-runs of *The Flavor of Love* on VH1. Karen walked into our bedroom and smiled slightly. She sat on the bed.

"Hey. What's up?"

"Nothing much. I was just waiting on you to get home. I didn't want to go to sleep without making sure that you made it home in one piece."

"Thank you, babe. I really appreciate that. How was the pizza?"

"It was alright. I invited Jay over to help me eat it."

"That's cool. Well, I am going to get into the shower real quick so that I can go to bed."

After that, Karen stood up and walked into the master bathroom and turned on the shower. Then she walked out of the bathroom and began to undress.

She took off everything except her bra and panties and walked toward the bathroom again. As she walked through the doorway of the bathroom, she unsnapped her bra.

At that moment, I could feel my blood start to supply the right organ. I jumped out of bed and trotted toward the bathroom. I also undressed as I got closer to the doorway. By the time that I was in the bathroom, I was as naked as a newborn baby. I was ready. Karen was already in the shower. I walked over to the bath tub and I eased back the shower curtain a little. Karen was just standing there in all of her nakedness, allowing the water from the shower to pour all over her hair and face. Her eyes were closed, and she was running her hands through her hair as the water soaked her. Karen's fair-skinned body was glowing like a model on the cover of a magazine. I could not take it anymore. I entered the shower and gently hugged her wet body.

"What are you doing? Not tonight, Tony! I am way too tired for this!"

Karen jerked from me as she was yelling at me. I just stood there, naked and shocked. I didn't know how to react to it.

"I was just trying to help you to relax a little."

"No, you were not! You were trying to satisfy your needs without thinking of mine. I told you how tired and stressful my day was and you still can only think about you."

"Now, isn't that the pot calling the kettle black. Do you even know how my day went? I tried to tell you about it, but it wasn't on your calendar to listen to me."

The tension in the shower was thick. The both of us were looking at the naked person like they were out of their mind. Karen was standing there beautifully angry, and I was standing there looking dumb, naked, and limp. I did not want to argue anymore. I made my surrendering exit out of the shower. I was wet and very disappointed. What did I do wrong? Sex always made *me* feel better. I was just trying to make *her* feel better. I dried off and put on my pajamas for the second time that night. My heart was beating fast, and my face was hot. I wanted to go off. I was trying to hold my anger.

Karen exited the bathroom about ten minutes later after I did. I could see the attitude on her face. She was wrapped in a towel like a ghetto burrito. She sat on the edge of the bed and put lotion on her body. This was not helping my situation at all. Karen looked over at me and spoke in a low and tired tone.

"I am very tired. My day was hell. I am sorry that I did not feel like being your little pleasure whore today."

Oh, no she didn't. My mouth dropped, and my head tilted to the side. "What the hell are you talking about? Where is all of this coming from?"

"Don't act like you don't know what I am talking about. I went to work early this morning, and I did not get home until eleven. Do you think that I want to have sex right now? I am tired out of my mind."

"I was trying to have sex with you. I wasn't asking you to run the mini marathon. Besides, the attitude is totally unnecessary. I had a long day also. You don't see me taking it out on you."

Then, in the middle of our conversation, her cell phone rang. She grabbed the phone off the dresser and answered it. Her attitude dropped immediately. She was talking in a mellow tone, and she was even smiling as she was talking to whoever it was on the phone. After a very short conversation, she hung up the phone.

"Who was that?"

"It was Tyson from work. He was making sure that I had gotten home."

"Well, the next time you talk to Tyson, let him know that it's not his job to make sure that you get home. It is mine."

"Don't even go there. Tyson was just being nice. We left work late, and he dropped me off at the parking garage."

"Oh, so you and Tyson are having a great time at work, huh? You are eating lunch together, you're riding in his car, and now he's calling you at midnight to check up on you."

"Tony, it is nothing like that. We just work together. Nothing more."

"Nothing more, huh? You know, all of a sudden, I'm not sleepy anymore."

I grabbed my pillow and headed for the living room. How could she sit there and nearly bite my head off in an argument, but as soon as Tyson calls, be happier than Tiger Woods in a Las Vegas brothel? Usually I wasn't a jealous guy, but Karen and Tyson were around each other all day at work. Then, they called each other all night, after work, to discuss so-called issues at work. It wasn't that I didn't trust Karen. I just didn't trust Tyson, or any other dude.

I really did not want to sleep on the couch, but I was so fired up that I had to get out of that bedroom. Besides, I was really pissed off that I couldn't get any loving. I just didn't see what the issue was. All she had to do was lay there and let me give her the best ten minutes of her life. I was willing to do all the labor. I just sat on the couch with my eyes open for about thirty minutes. My mind was racing. What was happening to us? Was this just a bad season that Karen and I were going through, or were we running out of love for each other? I still loved her, but I had grown very impatient over the past few months. When would it stop being about her and become about us? What about Laura? I finally fell asleep.

The next day, I woke up at about the same time that I was due at work. I was already late, and I hadn't even showered yet. On top of that, my head was pounding. I had a headache bigger than my last night's erection. It was nine o' clock, and Karen had already left for work without waking me up. I guess that it would be safe to assume that she was still upset from last night's altercation. I quickly brushed my teeth, jumped in the shower, got dressed, and ran out the door.

When I arrived at work, Jay was standing in the parking lot talking to a customer. He gave me a look that let me know the boss was looking for me. I was not even out of my car good when the sales manager approached me.

"Tony. I'm glad you decided to join us today."

"I am very sorry, Phil. I totally overslept, and my girl did not wake me."

"Is everything okay with you? You look like crap. Your clothes are wrinkled, and you haven't shaved in days."

"I'm fine, Phil."

"Maybe you should take the day off. Get yourself together and come to work tomorrow, ready to sell some inventory."

"No. I'm okay, Phil. I just—"

"It's not an option. I can't have you here looking like you got jumped in a dark alley. Go home and take care of yourself."

Phil walked off. I just sat in my car and held my head. What was happening to me? I was so embarrassed. I dialed Karen's number in my cell phone. As expected, it rang for a while, and then it was sent to her voicemail. Without any further thought at all, I reached for Laura's number, which I had placed in the glove box of my car. I dialed her number without any hesitation. She picked up on the first ring.

"Hello, this is Laura."

"Hello, Laura. It's Tony."

"Hey, Tony. What a surprise. It's good to hear from you. For a while there I didn't think that I was worthy of your phone conversation."

Laura didn't even try to hide the excitement in her voice. It was really good to hear her voice through that phone.

108

"So, are you working today?" I asked.

"Yes, I am. I just came out of a meeting, and I am typing an e-mail as we speak. What about you? Are you working today?

"Well, my plan was to work, but I'm not feeling very well. My manager gave me the rest of the day off."

"What's wrong? Is it anything serious?"

"No. I just got a huge headache."

"Where are you now?"

"I am still sitting in my car in the parking lot at the dealership."

"Which dealership do you work at?"

"I work at the BMW dealership over in Carmel."

"Oh, I know exactly where that is. I have an idea. How about I reschedule the rest of my meetings for the day so that I can bring you some medicine for your headache? We can meet at the Starbucks in Broad Ripple. A little caffeine might be good for your headache."

"I can't let you do that. I don't want to be a burden."

"Don't be silly. You could never be a burden to me. Besides, I asked you. You didn't ask me."

"Okay, how long will it take you to get over there?"

"Well, my office is located in Fishers, so I can be there in about a half."

"Good. I'll see you then."

"I'm on my way."

After we ended the call, I actually felt a little better. That was so easy and painless. I no longer had to carry that heavy number around in my pocket anymore. I had made the call. The funny part about it was, I didn't feel guilty about it. It was innocent. Laura offered to take care of me without my even having to ask her. It was really good to talk to her again. It was almost as if we never lost contact with each other. I closed my phone and headed to the Broad Ripple Starbucks.

17 Tyson

Last night ended the way that I wanted. I woke up this morning and rolled over to stare face to face with a beautiful woman. Joan was still asleep when I awoke. She was just as beautiful asleep as she was awake. As usual, it was a sensual night. Joan got to my loft about twenty minutes after I had gotten home. She arrived in her pajamas since it was so late. We talked for a few minutes before I stripped her out of her pajamas and gave her the business.

I was not much for conversation last night. For some reason, I couldn't get Karen out of my mind. I kept thinking about how excited she was when I gave her my parking pass. It was like she was not used to being treated like a woman. Maybe her fiancé was not treating her as well as she would like to be treated. Maybe there was room for me to squeeze into her life. I could use a woman like her on my team. Karen was smart, determined, driven, and sexy as hell. Don't get me wrong, Joan was a knockout also. But Karen was on another level. She already had a career. Karen was a future CEO in the making. Joan, on the other hand, had her entire life ahead of her. She was a blank canvass ready to receive her Picasso. I just didn't know if I was willing to help her paint it or not. It was hard enough guiding my own career. I couldn't imagine doing it all over for someone else's career.

I hopped out of bed and headed to the bathroom. I turned the hot water in the shower to full pressure. I just stood underneath the rain shower and let the water spray my scalp. I was trying to clear my mind to make room for the many obstacles I was sure to face at work. I couldn't have thoughts of Karen using up vital brain cells. I had to get my mind right. I had to focus. It was at that moment that I felt Joan's gentle hands touch my shoulder. I turned around and Joan was standing in the shower with me in all of her nakedness. This was sure to clear my mind, among other things.

***

I arrived at work, and it was business as usual. People were moving around quickly, putting out small fires. The phones were ringing off the hook. When I got to my desk, I had five messages on my work voicemail. Two were from Karen, and the other three were from some coworkers who were helping me with today's photo shoot for one of the ads. As I was checking my voicemail, Karen walked into my office.

"Where have you been?"

"Oh, I just got here."

"Well, it's good to see that someone was able to sleep in today."

"I wouldn't necessarily call it sleeping in."

"What do you mean?"

"Nothing."

I wore a devilish grin as I said that. My mind was on what really happened back at the loft. I quickly switched channels and began to talk about the shoot. Karen was looking good as usual. She had on a white blouse and black slacks. Karen was also wearing black heels and a red belt. I complimented her on her attire, and she brushed it off like she usually does when I compliment her. I could tell by the look in her eyes that she wanted to send a compliment my way. I was cleaner than a white dinner napkin. I had on my beige suit and my caramel-colored dress shoes. My dress shirt was light blue, and my tie was caramel colored also, with thin, blue stripes. If I didn't already know me, I would have thought that I was a model on page 36 of *GQ* magazine.

Since I felt so good and cleansed from this morning's water ride, I thought that I should look the part. I felt like I was the only man at the office that had gotten some loving this morning. As I walked through the row of cubicles on the way to my office, I could see the look of envy on the other men's faces. They looked so depressed and lacking. I was smiling, and I had an extra bounce in my step. My testicles were empty, and I felt light on my feet. As I walked past the other losers, I just nodded my head to let them know that, yes, I did get me some this morning, and it was good.

"Hello...Are you listening to me?"

Karen's voice brought me back to the present.

"Of course I'm listening. When is the photographer coming?"

"He is here now. He and the models are upstairs waiting on you as we speak. I suggest that you follow me upstairs so that we can get started with the shoot, unless you would like to stay here and continue with your daydreaming."

"I'm right behind you."

I could tell that Karen was in one of her moods. She didn't have much to say to me on the elevator ride up to the seventh floor. When we arrived at the photo shoot, everyone began to scatter and get into their places to begin working. It was known that

114

when both Karen and I walked into a room, things were going to get done. Karen immediately started talking to the models to give them direction as to how she wanted them to pose during the shoot. I headed over to the photographer and gave him directions as to what we wanted this ad to demonstrate. Throughout the entire process, Karen and I were the point of contact. Everyone involved in the photo shoot was asking us for guidance. I consulted Karen on many ideas that I had thought of for the ad, and she threw ideas my way as well.

We were running the photo shoot like true professionals. At one moment, I noticed my manager in the background observing how things were going. Karen and I were both engrossed in multiple tasks. When I looked back over at the area where my manager was standing, he was gone. I guess that he saw that Karen and I were handling things as we should. The actual shoot took most of the morning to complete. After all of the photographs were taken, we headed to the editing room to perform some magic. Karen sent everyone back to their desks with assigned tasks to complete. Karen and I sat with the photographer and went over the photos.

I called in our web designer and got her involved in the process also. We decided that it would be a good idea to use some of the photos on Weber's website as well as in some magazine ads. We had been working all day before I even looked up at the clock on the wall. It was seven o' clock in the evening, and we were still at it. The photographer had already left as well as our web designer, and Karen and I were working hard as usual. When I glanced across the table, Karen was rubbing her eyes with her index finger and her thumb. I could relate to what she was feeling. My eyes were so tired that I could barely read what was on the LCD screen on my laptop.

"We must both be crazy, huh?"

Karen looked up at me as if she had forgotten I was in the room with her.

"What do you mean?"

"You know, working long and late hours to chase our dreams. Risking health and home to make it to that next level, and then having to do it all over again and work even harder."

Karen smiled as if she were on the witness stand under oath and had been found guilty as charged.

"I guess you're right. We have to be crazy, both of us. I just feel as if I am almost there. I can see the goal right in front of my face. For so many years, I was just running in place, but now I can actually see that I am finally gaining some traction."

It was then that I realized Karen and I were both after the same thing. We both were hungry for the same success. Karen and I had been fighting the corporate machine for so long that we were ready for war. We were both ready for whatever obstacles we had to face head on and eat them alive like a kid picking his nose.

"Hey, I got an idea."

Karen looked at me as if I was up to something.

"What's your big idea, Tyson?"

"Well, first you have to tell me if you have anywhere that you need to be in the next couple of hours."

Karen looked at me suspiciously. "What does that have to do with anything?"

"Just answer the question. Do you have anything to do or not?"

"No, Tyson, I do not. Why do you ask?"

"Well, I wanted to know if you would like to watch a movie."

"What movie? Are you crazy? I am not about to go to the movies this late."

I started to laugh as I reached for my wallet and my laptop bag. I reached inside my laptop bag and pulled out three DVDs.

"I wasn't talking about taking you to the movies. I was talking about us watching one of the movies that I brought. We could watch one on my laptop. Everyone is gone home for the day, and we have been working nonstop. I was thinking that maybe you and I could head down the hall to the snack machine, grab as many goodies as we can, and come back and watch a movie. We need a way to relax. I don't want either of us ending up in the hospital because of a stroke or something."

Karen hesitated. I could tell that she was trying to see if I had an angle for my kindness.

"Sure, why not? You're right. We both could use a good movie. What will it be?"

"Let's see, I have *Brown Sugar*, *Love & Basketball*, and *The Best Man*. Which would you like to see?"

"Let's make it *Brown Sugar*."

"*Brown Sugar* it is."

We headed down the hall to get our treats for the movie. I got some M&M's and a bottled water. Karen got a Snickers candy bar and a Sprite. When we got back to the editing room, I started the movie in my laptop. Karen sat next to me at the table, and I placed the laptop on the table between us. We both had already seen that movie a thousand times before, so we carried on conversations with each other while we watched. At times we would stop talking and watch our favorite scenes of the movie and, at other times, we would laugh and carry on with our conversation.

The movie was over at about nine o' clock. Karen and I packed up all of our stuff and headed for the elevators. When we got outside of the office building, it was dark and warm. I stretched and yawned. Karen did the same. I walked Karen over to my old parking spot where her car was parked.

"Well, I guess that I will see you in the morning," I said.

"Where do you think you are going? I can't let you walk to the garage. Now it's my turn to give you a ride to your car, and don't even try to talk me out of it. I insist."

"Since you put it that way, I guess I don't have much of a choice."

Karen unlocked her side of the car and, once she got inside, she reached over to my side and unlocked the door for me. I got into her car, and she drove me to the parking garage over on Meridian Street. It was a short drive. When we arrived at the parking garage, I thanked her for the ride and told her to have a good night. I watched her as she drove off.

18 Tony

I arrived at Starbucks in about ten minutes. I looked at myself in the mirror of the sun visor in my car. Phil was right. I looked like crap. I grabbed my brush out of the armrest of the car and brushed my hair. I even tried to brush my goatee a little. I was open to anything that I could do to enhance my crusty appearance. As far as my wrinkled clothes, that was something that I could not fix. I got out of my car and made my way into Starbucks. It wasn't as crowded as it normally was because of the time of day. Laura was not there yet due to her longer drive. I grabbed a table close to the window and sat down. I scanned the room. Not far from where I was sitting, a young college-aged girl typed away on her laptop. At the table next to the college girl was an older couple. They were both sharing a newspaper and drinking coffee. The older woman looked to be in her sixties with curly white hair. The older gentleman was bald on top and had an island of white hair on the sides and back of his scalp. I never saw them utter a single word to each other. It was like they were alone, but together.

I didn't know if this was a good thing or a bad thing. Maybe it was just how this married couple operated. Maybe they had been together for so many years that they didn't need conversation to communicate their love to each other. I would assume that after decades of being married to someone, you would know his or her every habit. You would know how that person was feeling, just by looking at his or her facial expressions. I wondered, after so many years of being married to someone, living with that person in the same household, sharing the same bed, the same family, the same money, did they still say to each other, "I love you"?

Or, maybe they were mad at each other. Maybe the old guy left the toilet seat up for the millionth time. Maybe he forgot to wash the ten-year-old Buick in the parking lot. This might be stretching it, but maybe the wife did something to piss the husband off. I know that women are never wrong, but maybe the recipe that she tried for the first time last night made dinner a disaster. It was probably the worst dinner the old guy had ever eaten, but, in spite of this, he still had to eat it and compliment her to avoid hurting her feelings. Or, even worse, if he pissed her off by telling her how bad that dinner was, he would have to hunt his own dinner for the rest of the week. Maybe the old guy knew that by not telling his wife that the dinner was terrible, he was running a risk of her making it again in a few weeks.

After ten minutes of sitting in my hand-selected booth at Starbucks, I started to think about Karen and Laura. I thought about how much I loved Karen and how I would never intentionally do anything to hurt her. Then, I thought about Laura and how if Karen ever found out that we were meeting today, it would hurt Karen. How would I begin to explain to Karen my reason for meeting Laura? There would be no reasonable excuse to tell her. I guess that I could tell Karen how I was confused about my feelings for Laura. I could tell her how much I was in love with Laura at one time and that if Laura never left, then Karen and I probably wouldn't be together. Sure, I bet that would go over really well.

This kind of thinking made me nervous. My palms began to sweat, and my stomach started to growl. This was not the hungry type of growl. It was the find-the-nearest-restroom-stall growl. My insides were disturbed. I needed relief. I scanned the coffee shop for a restroom. Of course it was on the other side of the restaurant. Time was running out. My body had to relieve itself, and it did not care if it was on a chair or a toilet. I stood up and began to walk the long

122

stretch across the room. I was trying not to make it obvious that I was clinching my butt cheeks together to stop the flow of Nestle that was trying to escape from the chocolate factory. I tried to walk as cool as possible. The whole time my forehead was glazed with sweat. Once I arrived at my sanctuary of release, I quickly ran to the last stall. I knew that it was wrong to use the handicap stall, but I liked it because it had the most room. (I don't think that I am alone in my preference for the last stall.) Whenever I'm in that last stall, the door handle gets pulled by every person who enters the restroom for bowel release. The last stall is like the VIP area of the restroom.

After I paid my tithe to the toilet god, I washed my hands and exited the restroom. As I was walking out of the restroom, I noticed Laura standing in the entrance of Starbucks. She was looking around the coffee shop trying to find me. I raised my arm to get her attention. When she noticed me, she shared that smile that I knew so well. Laura was looking good. She had on a long, brown skirt that hugged her hips and a matching brown blouse and tan-colored heels. Her hair was bobbed and draped just below her chin. As we got closer to each other, we both held out our arms for an embrace. As I hugged Laura, I took in a deep breath. Her familiar fragrance did not disappoint me.

"You look gorgeous."

"Awe, that was nice. Thank you. You always knew how to make me blush. You are looking good yourself, Mr. Tony."

"Thanks. Have you been here long?"

"No. I just got here. How long have you been here?"

"Oh, I have been here for a couple of minutes. I just went to the bathroom to wash my hands."

The older couple that I saw thirty minutes ago looked up at me in surprise when I said that.

Laura and I walked over to the table that I had previously selected. I pulled out her chair for her to sit down.

"No, you take a seat. I came here to make sure that you were alright. You are the one with the head-ache. You have a seat, and I'll go get the coffee. Do you have any requests?"

"I like my coffee dark and sweet."

"Oh, well I hope that I can fulfill that order."

We both laughed and Laura walked over to the counter to place the order. As she walked away from the table, I looked at her silhouette from the back. Baby girl was banging. Laura had a backside that put J-Lo's to shame. It was perfectly round with hips to match. To top it off, Laura had muscular thighs and calves. As she walked toward the counter, her high heels perfectly accented her calves. Laura also had a small waist and medium-sized breasts. When you put all of this together, it made a beautiful body. When we were dating, Laura and I would work out all of the time. We would get up early in the morning and go down to the canal and run. This was our thing. We would do it no matter what. Even if we were mad at each other and hated each other's guts, we would meet at the canal and run. Some nights, we would run around the parking lot at the hospital across the street from her old apartment community. We were a very healthy couple. All we ate was fish, chicken, and turkey.

Laura was in better shape now than she was when I last saw her. She started to walk back toward where I was sitting, carrying two cups of Starbucks crude. Laura sat my coffee in front of me and started to reach inside her purse. She pulled out a small bottle of Excedrin and shook two pills onto a napkin.

"Here you go, sir. We got you some caffeine and some medicine. This should knock out your headache in no time."

"Thanks, Laura. I really appreciate your doing this for me. You know that you didn't have to."

"You are welcome. Yes, I did have to. There is no way that I could have gone back to doing whatever it was I was doing after you informed me that you

125

were not feeling well. Besides, you sounded like a mess on the phone. I really believed that you were either sick or putting on an Oscar-winning performance."

Laura sat in the vacant chair across the table from me. She looked at me, smiled, and took a sip of her coffee. I smiled back in a shy, but smooth manner and downed my pills with a sip of my own coffee. While we were both sitting there, Laura's phone rang, but she didn't answer it. She sent it to voicemail and switched her phone to vibrate mode.

"I apologize for that. I usually have my phone on vibrate when I'm out of the office."

"No problem. I didn't even notice."

"So, Tony, aside from the headache, how is your day going so far?"

"Well, I haven't really done much today to even give a rating. Let's see, I woke up late. I arrived at work late, and I got sent home early. That about sums it up."

"Wow. That's quite a morning. The good part is that you still have enough time left in your day to make it better. I haven't done much either except for attending a meeting that started at seven o' clock this morning. I stopped over at Best Buy and picked up the new Alicia Keys CD on the way here. Have you heard it?"

"I heard a few of the singles on the radio, but I haven't heard the whole CD. I heard that it is really good, though. The single that they are playing on the radio now is really good."

"Are you talking about the one that she has with Common in the video?" she asked.

"Yeah, that's the one."

"I would have to agree with you on that one. That is a really touching song," she said.

I took another sip of my coffee. I felt my phone vibrating on my belt. I looked at the caller ID. It was Jay. I let it go to my voicemail.

"I bought a CD the other day," I said.

"Yeah, what did you get?"

"I bought Jill Scott's new CD."

"I got that one, too. I really like it. I was playing it this morning while I was getting dressed."

Laura and I sat in Starbucks for a couple of hours. Our conversations danced from one subject to another. We talked about more music, movies, and television shows. I had almost forgotten how much Laura and I had in common.

"Remember when you and I would watch *The Real World* on MTV together?" I asked.

"Oh my God! I can't believe that you remembered that. I remember when I first asked you to watch it with me; you told me that the show was for

127

girls. After a few shows, you were asking me when the next new episode was coming on. We watched every episode together with a bag of popcorn."

I started to look around the coffee shop to see if anyone was listening to our conversation.

"You might want to lower your voice. I don't want anyone in here knowing that you got me addicted to a reality show."

We both laughed. I couldn't remember the last time that I laughed like that. It felt good to be able to talk to someone with the same interests that I had. I must have laughed my headache out of my head because my head wasn't hurting anymore. Laura looked at the chrome watch that was dressing her arm.

"Look how time flies. We have been here for two hours. It doesn't seem like it's been that long. How's the headache?"

"It's good. I feel better. Thanks for helping me with that."

"No problem. Well, I think I'd better get out of here. I have some things to take care of before I head home. Is there anything else that you need from me?"

"No. You have done enough for me today already."

"Would you like to meet me for lunch tomorrow?"

"Sure. I can do that. Where would you like to meet?"

"I'll give you a call tomorrow morning sometime and let you know."

"It sounds like a plan."

We both stood up and walked out of the coffee shop and into the parking lot. I walked Laura to her car, and we hugged again. Laura smiled at me and eased into her car. I closed the driver-side door for her and walked across the lot to my car. Laura beeped her horn at me and waved as she pulled out of the parking lot.

Once I got into my car, I called Jay.

"Hello?"

"Jay, what's up?"

"Nothing much. What's up with you? Were you just faking sick to get the day off, or are you really sick?"

"I was sick this morning, but I'm feeling better now."

"Where are you? Are you at home?"

"Nope. I just left from having lunch with Laura."

"Laura? What is that all about? It looks like someone has rejuvenated the long-lost player that has been trapped inside of a shackled body. I didn't know that you still had it in you. I'm proud of you. I am also glad to see that some of my game has rubbed off on you."

"No. It was nothing like that. We just met for coffee and conversation. Laura and I are just friends. She knows about Karen and me, and she is respectful of that."

"Okay. If that's your story, I guess you have to stick to it."

I could tell that Jay didn't believe me at all. Jay remembered how tight Laura and I were back in the day. Knowing all that we had been through together, I probably wouldn't believe my story either.

19 Karen

I pulled into my apartment community at around ten o' clock. Once again, I was nearing the end of another late night at work. I hadn't spoken with Tony all day. I saw that I had a missed call from him earlier. I had planned to give him a call back, but time escaped me. As soon as I parked my car in front of my apartment building, I made sure that I called Tyson to let him know that I had made it home safely. I didn't want to have another argument with Tony because of another late-night call from Tyson. After calling Tyson, I grabbed my things out of the car and walked across the blacktopped parking lot to my building.

Once I got inside the apartment, I saw Tony sitting on the couch watching television. I placed my purse and laptop bag on the coffee table, and I sat next to Tony.

"Hey, babe."

"Hey, what's up?"

"Nothing. How was your day?"

"It was pretty good. How was yours?"

"Well, you already know the answer to that question. It was busy as usual, but I was able to finish the photo shoot that we had today."

"That's good to hear. I'm sure that you are glad to have that over with."

"Yes, I am."

Tony was in a better mood than I had expected him to be in. Last night we had that big argument, and we hadn't talked to each other all day. I was sure that I was in for another argument today. Maybe last night's argument was not as bad as I had thought. I still felt that it would probably be appropriate to settle things.

"Tony, I just wanted to tell you that I am sorry about last night. I was just so stressed from my long day, and I took it out on you."

"That's alright. I am partly the blame. Instead of jumping to conclusions about you and Tyson, I should have been more sensitive toward your needs. I love you very much, and there is no doubt in my mind that you love me, too."

I was very surprised at how well Tony handled everything. It was as if last night had never happened. He must have really had a good day today. He was usually this happy whenever he made lots of sales at the car lot. I knew that I had been sacrificing

132

quality time with Tony for work time, but if I didn't do the work, then someone else would. Lately, I had been spending more time with Tyson than I had with Tony. I could see how he was becoming frustrated by it. With all that said, it was still very important that he supported me through this process.

I didn't want to lose Tony. He was the best thing that had ever happened to me. He was more than a fiancé to me. Tony was my best friend, and losing him would be tragic. I gave Tony a soft kiss on his lips. After I kissed him, I smiled at him and stared into his eyes.

"I am the luckiest woman alive. Thank you for being here for me, Tony."

"You're welcome. I know it's late, but do you feel like staying up and watching a little television with me?"

"Sure. What's on?"

"Don't know, but I can check."

Tony grabbed the digital cable remote control and hit the guide button. He started to cycle through the movie channels to see if there was anything on that was worth watching. Then Tony's eyes showed excitement.

"Karen. Look what's on HBO tonight. *Brown Sugar* comes on in ten minutes. I haven't seen that movie in a long time. Let's watch it."

I began to choke on my own spit.

"Karen, are you alright?"

I couldn't believe it. Of all the nights that *Brown Sugar* could be playing, why tonight? Should I tell Tony that I had just watched the same movie about an hour ago with Tyson? We made up with each other less than five minutes ago, and already another argument might be in the making. I didn't know what to do. I did not know if I should tell Tony the truth or just act as if it had been a long time since I had seen the movie also. I knew that honesty was an important ingredient in a relationship, but I remembered reading somewhere that too much honesty was worse than no honesty. I didn't remember where I read that, but at that very moment I truly agreed with it.

"Okay. Let's watch it."

"Good, I can't wait until it starts."

"Me either."

We watched the entire movie. I could not believe that I was watching it for the second time in one night. The movie was so fresh in my mind that I could recite every scene if I wanted to. I started to get a little sleepy toward the end of the movie. I could feel myself trying to drift off into hibernation. Tony was wide awake through the entire movie. I tried my best to

134

seem interested in the movie, but my body was running out of fuel.

I was awakened by Tony at midnight. He helped me off the couch and guided me into our bedroom. Tony helped me out of my work clothes, and he grabbed a nightgown out of one of my dresser drawers, and handed it to me. He helped me ease into my nightgown, and then he covered my body with the blankets that we had on our bed. After he tucked me in, Tony turned off the lights and started to walk back toward the living room.

"Where are you going?"

"I'm not that sleepy, so I am going to watch a little television before I come to bed."

"That's fine. Thank you for tucking me in."

"You're welcome. Good night."

"Good night, babe."

Shortly after that, I was fast asleep.

***

The beeping got louder and louder. Finally, I was awake and reaching for my cell phone. It was seven o' clock, and it felt like I had been asleep for only a couple of minutes. I looked at the caller ID, and it was Tyson. Before I answered the phone, I looked over at Tony on his side of the bed, but he was still sleeping.

"Hello?"

My voice sounded like I was the baritone sing-
er for the Temptations.

"Hello, Karen. Did I wake you?"

"Of course you woke me. It's seven in the
morning."

"Well, I am sorry if I interrupted your beauty
rest, but you are aware that we have a meeting with
the managers at eight, right?"

"Oh my God. I totally forgot about that. Can
you cover me until I get there?"

"Of course. I'll get the meeting started and try
to stall them until you arrive, but you have to hurry."

"I will. I am getting up now. I will see you
when I get there."

"Okay. Bye."

"Bye."

I hopped out of bed and started to get ready to
leave. After my shower, I walked back into the bedroom. Tony was awake and was just getting out of
bed.

"Good morning, babe." I kissed him on the
cheek.

"Good morning."

"I was just about to wake you," I told him.

Tony sat on the edge of the bed and watched
me as I was getting ready. He yawned a couple of
times and rubbed his eyes. I went back into the bath-

room and brushed my teeth and did a quick job on my hair. I then sat next to Tony on the bed and started to rub lotion on my body.

"Do you have another long day today?"

"Yes, it is looking that way. I am already running late for a meeting, and I have some other deadlines that are coming up."

"Yeah, I need to get up myself. I have to be at work in an hour. Do you think that you are going to be working late again tonight? If not, I was hoping we could go out to dinner or something."

"I don't know if I will be able to. I am sure that I will probably be working late, and I don't want to stand you up. I'm sorry."

"No problem. I kind of figured that you might have to work late anyway. We can go out some other time."

I really felt bad about telling Tony no, but I already knew that I would be running a risk of not being able to get off work in time to make it to dinner. It had been like that for a while now. I just did not know what the day had in store for me. Shortly after our conversation, I was on my way to work.

The morning traffic was terrible. People were driving like mental patients. Cars were dipping in and out of lanes without warning. Horns were being honked every other minute. In the middle of all this confusion, I was trying to apply my makeup in the rear-view mirror and drive at the same time. Interstate 70 was usually wide open, but it was very congested today. This gave me time to think and plan my day. After my meeting with the managers, I had to call the Weber execs and set up a meeting with them for tomorrow. I also had to meet with our web designer to make sure she would be ready for the launch.

I arrived at my office building later than I expected. I quickly parked my car in my newly attained parking space and jetted to the elevator. Once I made it upstairs, I could see Tyson conducting the meeting through the windows of the conference room. I quickly straightened my hair and my clothes and entered the conference room.

20 Tyson

The past few weeks had been crazy. Karen and I had been working nonstop. We were at the office late every day this week. I was getting to work at around eight in the morning but was not leaving earlier than nine in the evening. I was actually able to spend lots of time with Joan through it all. She had been at my loft every day this week. Joan had done a good job of making sure that I was eating a good dinner after my long, stressful days.

Last night Joan met me at my loft and made me some grilled chicken and macaroni. I have to admit, she really knew her way around the kitchen. I don't think I had ever eaten a meal as good as the one that she made for me. She really laid out the red carpet for me. Joan wouldn't even let me get off the couch. She carried on a conversation with me from the kitchen while I relaxed. We listened to some old-school music that was playing through the Bose speakers installed throughout my loft. Joan told me about the interviews that she was assigned to do during her college's upcoming homecoming. I could tell that she was pretty excited about it because she would get to interview all of the performers before and after the live concert.

The aroma of tastefully seasoned chicken invaded my nostrils. As soon as the chicken's aroma hit me, my stomach started to growl. My body was ready to devour that savory poultry. My mouth watered at the thought of chewing the tender meat. Joan brought my meal out to the living room. I tried to get off the couch, but she insisted that I sit still and enjoy my meal. She poured me a fresh glass of lemonade that she had recently made. I felt like a king. All of my worries of the day were gone. I was eating a fine meal, prepared by some fine hands. Joan grabbed a place next to me, and we ate our meal together. I was starving. Time went by so fast at work that I didn't get a chance to eat anything for lunch. The meal that was prepared especially for me hit the spot.

After we finished our meal, I was stuffed. I couldn't move if I wanted to. I just smiled and gave Joan a greasy kiss on her cheek. Frankie Beverly was singing through the speakers, and chicken and macaroni were flowing through my digestive tract. To top it all off, I was enjoying some quality time with a fine young woman. A man couldn't ask for much more than that.

Shortly after we finished our meal, Joan went back into the kitchen.

"Where are you going?"

"I'm not done yet. I am going to make us some drinks."

Joan mixed up a couple of glasses of Amaretto Sour. They were mixed to perfection. The drink made by my sexy visitor reminded me of when I would have a few while gambling on the casino boats at the harbor in Gary. I really enjoyed the type of attention and pampering that Joan was supplying me. I could tell that she was starting to really fall for me. I could also say that the feeling was mutual.

We both sipped on our specialty drinks as we conversed. I was still sitting on the couch, and Joan was sitting on the floor. She had on blue jeans and a pink polo shirt. Joan's back was leaning against the couch, and her legs were crossed. Her bare feet were exposed, showing off her new pedicure. Joan's feet looked soft. It was obvious that she had never played a sport in her life. There wasn't a sign of a corn or a bunion in sight. Her feet were small, and her toes were short with French-tip accents. We talked and laughed. Then, we laughed and talked. It was a relaxing night for me.

I woke up around three in the morning to the sound of Sade's sultry rhythms resonating throughout my loft. I was lying on the hardwood floor of my living area, and Joan was asleep on my chest. There were two empty wine glasses within reach. I gently ran my fingers through Joan's natural mane, and she slowly opened her eyes. When she realized that it was me she was looking at, Joan introduced me to a bashful smile. I kissed her on her forehead, and she started to work her way off the floor. Joan held out her hand to help me off the floor also. Once I was on my feet, I told Joan to head upstairs; I turned off the lights that we had left on all night, and I also powered down the sound system. After my tasks, I headed upstairs, and I eased onto the bed next to Joan. We were both asleep within minutes.

21 Tony

Laura and I had been meeting for lunch every weekday for a couple of weeks now. We had met at various places to satisfy our midday appetites. Sometimes Laura drove to my side of town to meet me for lunch, and on others I drove to her side of town to meet her. It had all been pretty innocent up to this point. We'd just sit and laugh and talk while we ate our meals. We discussed everything from politics to the latest movies. Laura told me all about her position that she had while in Texas. She explained how hot it was out there compared to Indiana. Laura explained that, for the most part, she enjoyed living in Texas. She said it was much different from Indiana, but she liked it.

Laura had been on my mind a lot lately. I sometimes wondered why I didn't get along with my fiancée as well as I did with her. I usually had alone time whenever I was at home. Of course, this was not by choice. Karen usually didn't stroll in until around nine o' clock at night during these days. I tried to make the days go by faster by meeting Jay at the gym after work or even by going to the mall and doing a little window shopping. The working out had really been a stress reliever for me. Between the working out and the lack of sex, I could probably rip a phone book in half with my bare hands. As for dinner, I had ordered so many pizzas that the delivery guy and I had become friends. I was helping him plant some shrubs at his home next week.

My thoughts were interrupted by the sight of Laura walking through the front doors of her office building. As usual, she looked great. Laura smiled as soon as her eyes found my position in the parking lot. Laura was wearing a gray, one-button, tweed skirt suit. Her ensemble was highlighted with a pair of black Nine West stretch boots that hugged her calves. Her confident and sexy stroll led her to the passenger's side of my car. I was holding the door open for her as she approached. Laura greeted me with a quick embrace and another smile. After Laura claimed her place inside my car, I closed the car door and made my way back to the driver's side. Laura had already opened the door for me from the inside. As I sat inside the car, Laura began to speak.

"Thank you for picking me up for lunch."

"You're welcome. By the way, you are looking really nice today."

144

Laura smiled and touched my hand.

"Thank you. You always compliment me whenever you see me. I think that is so sweet."

"I just state the obvious."

"Whatever."

"No, really. You are always dressed nice when I see you. Any man would be a fool not to recognize that. Besides, I'm sure that I am not the only man who has complimented you today."

"No, you are not the only man who has complimented me today, but when you compliment me, I know that you really mean it. Enough about me, you are looking rather handsome yourself. Did you have to work today?"

"Sure did. I have to be back at work in an hour."

"Oh. So we better get going for lunch. What do you have a taste for?"

"I figured we could stop at Einstein Bagels and grab a bite to eat."

"I don't have any objections to that idea."

Once we arrived at Einstein's, we selected a table by one of the windows inside the restaurant. We placed a few of our belongings on the table and headed to the counter to order our meals. I ordered an Italian chicken panini, and Laura ordered the turkey club panini. For drinks, I ordered myself a caffe latte, and

Laura ordered a caramel macchiato. I suggested to Laura that she grab us some napkins as I paid for our meals and carried the tray to our table.

After we both took our places at the table by the window, I said grace, and we began to eat.

"Thank you for paying for my lunch. I insist that I pay for the next one."

"I insist that you do also."

We both laughed as Laura tossed one of her napkins in my direction. She knew that I was joking. Laura was accustomed to me occasionally teasing her.

"How is your day going at the car lot today?"

"It's going alright. We haven't had much traffic this morning, but hopefully it will pick up this afternoon."

"I hope that it does pick up for you, but if it doesn't then we'll just have to start bringing a lunch to work with us."

"I see that you have a few jokes in you this morning, huh?"

Laura and I continued to eat our lunches and share a few laughs. When we were done with our meals, I dropped Laura back off at work, and I headed back to the BMW lot.

22 Tony

I spoke with Karen earlier today, and she told me that she and a few of her coworkers were going out tonight as a stress reliever. She invited me to come along, but none of her other coworkers were bringing their spouses, so I opted out. The last thing that I wanted to do was to go out with them and be totally oblivious to all of their work-related jokes and conversations. I told her that I would probably go somewhere with Jay and hang out. I needed a beer like a stripper needed a dollar.

Laura called my cell phone.

"Hello?" I answered.

"Hello, may I speak to Tony?"

"Speaking."

"Hi. Are you busy?"

"Nope. I was just sitting here, trying to figure out what I am going to do tonight. Karen is going out with some of her coworkers, and I really don't feel like sitting in the house tonight."

"Well, that is actually the reason that I called. A friend of mine plays in a band, and they are playing at the Vitesse tonight. I know how you like to hear live music, so I was calling to see if you would like to go and hear them play."

"That actually sounds like a pretty good idea. What time are they playing?"

"They should be on stage around nine o' clock or so."

I was all for it. I really liked jazz and blues music. Any chance that I got to hear it live was a chance that I was willing to take. It was perfect timing. Karen was out with her coworkers, and she probably wouldn't be home until late. I had already told Karen that I would probably go somewhere with Jay, so all I had to do was get Jay to back me up on my story. I hated that I had to sneak, but there was no way that Karen would believe that Laura and I going out was innocent.

I accepted Laura's offer, and I told her that I would pick her up at her townhouse at half past eight. After I hung up with Laura, I called Jay and informed him of the night's events. After a few jokes and laughs, he agreed to back me up. As soon as I got off the phone with Jay, I took a quick shower and got dressed. I was cleaner than the Board of Health. I had on my Kenneth Cole cognac loafers and a pair of dark brown, double-pleated dress pants. My upper body was covered with a beige, v-neck sweater with a dark brown-and-white striped dress shirt underneath. I was freshly shaven, and my hair was faded. I smelled like the cologne counter at Macy's, and I was looking good. If I didn't already know me, I would ask me for my phone number.

I stopped by Mike's Car Wash on the way to Carmel to pick up Laura. I had to get my car prepared for tonight's events. After getting my car washed, I cruised in and out of lanes on Interstate 465 to the tunes of the O'Jays playing through my car speakers. I was feeling cool and laid back. My head was bobbing slowly with the music, and my mind was at ease.

The address and directions that Laura had given me led me to the Villages of West Clay. This was a newly developed area in Carmel that had Charleston, South Carolina-influenced architecture wrapping every house and townhome. I drove past the stately and historical-looking homes until I reached the townhome with the numbers on the mailbox that matched the ones I had written on my paper. I parked my recently washed car and walked on the sidewalk to Laura's front door with my smoothest glide. I rushed a piece of minty bubble gum into my mouth, and then I pressed the doorbell. I could hear Laura's voice telling me that she was coming to the door. Soon after

149

that, the red door to her townhome slowly opened and exposed the sexy owner of the residence. Laura was looking flawless. She had on a black, long-sleeved, fitted dress that stopped just above her knees. It hugged every curve on her body like a latex glove. She was holding a small, red Chanel purse with a gold buckle. Laura was also wearing a pair of high-heeled Chanel pumps with black and red straps. Her makeup was applied with perfection, and her overall look was breathtaking.

After I took in all of her beauty, Laura brought me back to reality with a hug.

"Aren't we looking handsome tonight."

"Thanks. I must say, you are looking gorgeous."

"Why thank you, Tony."

"Are you ready to leave?"

"As ready as I can get."

I held Laura's hand and guided her down the steps of her front porch. I then rushed to open the passenger door of my car and waited until she was situated inside before I closed it. It took us about thirty minutes to reach the Vitesse. We sat on a brown, leather sofa in the back corner of the lounge. One of the live bands was already playing on stage. The lights were low, and the crowd was thick. I could hear the buzz of multiple conversations going on in the background and live, smooth music coming from the front of the lounge. When the thin, red-haired waitress with wide hips approached our area, I ordered a Long Island iced tea, and Laura ordered an apple martini.

"Tony, you are looking really good tonight. I almost forgot how well you clean up."

"Are you flirting with me, Ms. Laura?"

Laura laughed and took a sip of her apple martini. I watched as the fluid rushed into her mouth through her slightly parted lips.

"No, I'm not. I am just stating the obvious."

"Well, I thank you. But, I must say, you are looking amazing yourself. I couldn't pick out a flaw if I tried."

It was obvious that we were both still very attracted to each other. I could tell by the way that Laura looked at me that she was still attracted to me. There was no uncertainty that I was attracted to her. I think that it would be safe to say that every male in the lounge was attracted to Laura. We talked and flirted with each other the whole time that we were at the Vitesse.

Laura's friend's band made their way to the stage. Her friend was the vocalist. Laura's friend sang her band's rendition of Lauryn Hill's "Ex-Factor." It was amazing. Her voice filled the room. You could

151

hear the pain and love experience in her voice as she sang. The band backed her up to perfection. As Laura spoke to me, my mind would drift. It would drift to the past when Laura and I were an item. I remembered the times that we would go out on the weekends and have all kinds of fun. It didn't matter where we were going, as long as we were together. Whether it was shooting pool at the downtown BW3's or playing the arcade games at Jillian's, we always had a good time.

Back then, it was a challenge for us to keep our hands off each other. We had sex all the time—every night before we went to sleep. If we were alone and we were together, then chances are we were ripping each other's clothes off. I don't think that I had ever been that attracted to any other woman in my life.

As the music played in the background, and as Laura was talking to me, I noticed a familiar feeling. It was a feeling of bliss and lure. Being around Laura made me happy again. As she spoke, I stared into her eyes, wishing that I was single. I wanted to kiss Laura so badly that my mouth was watering. She wasn't making it easy for me either. Laura was sitting close to me with her legs crossed in my direction. As we talked, she would occasionally place her hand on my thigh or lightly run her fingertips from my temple to my chin. She would do that back when we were dating, and it drove me crazy. It still did. I continued to order Long Island iced teas to calm my nerves. Laura wasn't drinking that much, but I was. I told the wide-hipped red-head to keep the drinks coming.

"Laura. I don't mean to bring a cloud over our night, but I have a question that I have to ask you that has been burning my insides."

"What is it?"

"Well, the past couple of weeks have been kind of crazy. We have been meeting almost every day for lunch. We've had long conversations on the phone, and now we are hanging out and having drinks together. I'm not complaining about any of it. As a matter of fact, I have been having a really good time with you, and tonight has been awesome. I'm just curious, why did you leave?"

I could tell that the subject of the conversation had turned uncomfortable for Laura. She sucked in her bottom lip, and her eyes looked over the room. Laura then looked me in the eyes and forced herself to speak.

"It is funny that you asked me that. I knew that the day was coming when you would ask me. I have asked myself the same question over the past couple of weeks. Every time that I come up with a reason as to why I left, I begin to feel dumb because no reason validates my leaving you. I guess you could say that I left because I could feel us drifting apart. We were arguing a lot, and we weren't spending much time together anymore. I could feel a real disconnect with you. You went from spending every night with me to just a couple of nights a week. I guess I knew that the big breakup was on the way, and it was easier for me to leave than to see you with another woman."

As Laura spoke to me, her eyes were starting to produce tears. I could see both hurt and regret in her face. She held my left hand with both of her hands. The band was playing their version of Luther Vandross' "Love Won't Let Me Wait." I wanted Laura more than ever. My mouth was watering so bad that I could eat a whole jar of peanut butter and not even blink. My entire body was covered with goose bumps. I reached out and pulled Laura close to me. Then, I hugged her. I held her for what felt like forever. I took in a deep breath and inhaled the scent of her perfume, that very perfume that had haunted my nostrils for years. I rested my face in her neck. I held her for what felt like eternity. I could feel my eyes starting to water as I held the woman that I was once in love with. After our embrace, I gently pulled back from Laura and wiped her tears from her cheek. She placed her hand on the side of my face and smiled. I raised my hand and motioned for the red-haired waitress to bring me another drink.

154

23 Tony

After a few hours and many glasses of Long Island iced tea, I was officially drunk. Laura didn't even finish the one drink that she had ordered when we first arrived at the Vitesse. I, on the other hand, ordered well over seven drinks. It was all that I could do in order to keep my paws off Laura. I was so tipsy that I could barely walk straight. I had the red-head waitress close out my tab, and I left her a hefty tip. Laura had to help me walk out of the Vitesse. I had my arm around her shoulders, and she wrapped her arm around my waist as we walked to my car. Of course I was too far gone to even think about getting behind the wheel of my car, so Laura drove us back to her townhouse.

During the drive back to Carmel, all kinds of thoughts were going through my mind. How would I get back home? I couldn't have Laura drop me off. That would have been a big mistake. There no way that I could have pulled that off. I couldn't drive myself home. The last thing that I needed on my mind was to kill an innocent motorist because of my irresponsibility.

About forty minutes later, we arrived at Laura's townhome. She looked over at me in the passenger side of my car.

"You are welcome to stay here if you need to. I have a guest room that you could sleep in."

"I think that I am going to take you up on that offer, but I have to make a couple of phone calls first."

I called Jay and let him know what was going on. I gave him Karen's number and told him to call and tell her that I was over at his apartment, passed out drunk. Jay jokingly accepted the task, and I was in the clear. I wasn't trying to be sneaky. I just felt like I didn't have a choice. I was stranded way out in Carmel.

Laura helped me out of the car and up the stairs of her front porch. She leaned me against the red door of her townhome as she unlocked the door. After unlocking the door, Laura helped me inside and allowed me to fall face first onto the microfiber couch in her living room. I rolled over onto my back and stared at the textured ceiling. My eyes surveyed the room. I noticed the walnut-colored bamboo hardwood flooring that started in the living room and continued into the kitchen. Craftsman brown walls encased the first floor. A forty-two-inch LCD television

156

stared at me from above the mantel of a natural-stone fireplace. Laura walked past my view of the room, and she kicked off her shoes and placed her purse and keys on the end table.

"Come on. Let's get you upstairs."

Laura grabbed both of my arms and helped me to my feet. She then led the way upstairs to the guest bedroom of her townhome. Laura gently helped me onto the bed. As soon as I was on my back, the room began to spin, and I was sweating out of control. All of the drinks that I had downtown were really starting to catch up with me. I could feel Laura taking off my shoes. Then, she helped me out of my shirt and sweater. Laura then left the bedroom and returned a few moments later with a cool, wet towel. She lay close to me and began to rub my face and neck with the towel. It was so soothing and tranquil. My mind was overcome with memories of how she used to take care of me whenever I was sick. Laura continued to wipe my face in gentle strokes.

***

I awoke the next morning with a killer headache. My mouth was dryer than the turkey that Karen cooked last Thanksgiving. I grabbed my forehead and opened my eyes. That's when I realized that I was still at Laura's place. I looked to my right, and Laura was lying there sound asleep. It was at that moment that I noticed that my shirt was off. I sat up so fast that all of the blood in my head slammed against the front of my skull. The pain was paralyzing. I immediately looked to see if I still had my pants on. I was more than relieved to find that not only were they still on, but they weren't even unbuckled. I looked over at Laura again, and she was still fully dressed, except for her shoes. That was a relief. I smirked and exhaled as if I had dodged a bullet. The last thing that I wanted to do was to cheat on Karen. I sat on the side of the bed with my feet touching the frieze carpet of Laura's brightly colored guest bedroom.

I slipped on my socks and shoes that were located next to the bed. I then stood up and put on my shirt. I threw my sweater over my shoulder as I checked my pockets for my keys.

"They're on the nightstand. Your keys fell out of your pocket when you were on the couch."

In my urgency to get dressed, I must have made too much noise. Laura was awake and looking at me. I hoped that I didn't look as scared and confused as I felt.

"How are you feeling?"

"Aside from the eight hundred-pound gorilla punching me in the back of the head, I feel okay."

"Hangover, huh?"

"You guessed it. I have to get going. I didn't mean to sleep that long."

"Are you in trouble?"

"I don't think so."

I grabbed the rest of my things and headed downstairs. Laura opened the front door for me, and I walked out onto the porch. She followed me onto the porch and stood there barefoot, with folded arms. The sun was beaming down on us. I closed my eyes as the bright sunlight intensified my headache. I gave Laura a quick hug, and then I made my journey to my car. Once in my car, I looked at the porch that I had just left, and Laura was still standing there. She was watching me leave. The look on her face described exactly how I was feeling. Not how my head was feeling, but how I felt about the whole situation. I didn't want to leave. It's not that I didn't want to get back home to Karen, but I didn't want what I felt last night to end. I was back in reality. Playtime was over, and it was time to go home. It was like the feeling that you get on the night of your birthday. It is 11:58 p.m., and your day is over in two minutes. In two minutes, you are no longer the focus of attention. In two minutes, you are a regular person again.

24 Karen

As soon as I awoke this morning, I noticed that Tony wasn't home yet. Jay called my cell last night to inform me that the two of them were drinking heavily and that Tony couldn't hang. Jay said that Tony was passed out on his couch. This had happened before, so I was not surprised.

The sun would not let me sleep any longer, so I got out of my queen-sized bed and headed to the kitchen to prepare a fresh pot of coffee. My movements were sluggish, and my eyelids were puffy. I really had a good time last night with my coworkers. It was a night of good drinks and colorful conversations.

On my way to the kitchen, my cell rang. I thought that it would be Tony informing me that he was on his way home, but it was Stacey. I pressed the BlackBerry cell phone against the side of my face.

"Hello?"

"Hey girl, what's up?"

"Nothing much. Just woke up. I was wondering where you have been. I haven't heard from you in a few days. What have you been up to?"

"Girl, nothing exciting. Just working and paying bills. Is everything alright between you and Tony?"

Stacey sounded concerned. I could tell that something was on her mind. She rarely called me that early in the morning. She was usually worn out from the party-filled night before.

"Yeah, everything is alright. We have had a few arguments, but nothing out of the ordinary. Why do you ask?"

"Is he home right now?"

"Nope. He and Jay went out last night and got drunk, so Tony stayed over at Jay's apartment. He should be home sometime this morning."

"Does Jay still live over in Westlake apartments, on the west side of town?"

"As far as I know, he still does. Why?"

"Well, I'm not trying to get anything started between the two of you. You know that I like Tony, and I think he is a great guy…"

"Stacey, get on with it. I know that Tony is a great guy, but what is on your mind?"

"Well, I just saw Tony leaving a townhome on the north side of town, in the Carmel area."

161

I stopped what I was doing in the kitchen, and I leaned against the refrigerator. What Stacey said obviously sparked my interest. There was no way that Tony was on the north side of town. He didn't have any friends that lived on the north side of town, at least not any friends that I was aware of. Stacey had to be wrong on this one.

As I was talking to Stacey on my cell phone, Tony walked into our apartment. I made sure to mask the conversation that I was having with Stacey. Tony kissed me on my cheek and headed to the bedroom. As soon as I saw Tony disappear into the bedroom, I continued my conversation with Stacey.

"Are you sure that it was him?"

"Karen, I am almost positive that it was Tony. Last night, I went out with one of my male friends. Well, first we went to see that new Tyler Perry movie. It was really good. You should go see it. Then, we went to dinner, and one thing led to another and…"

"Stacey! Get to the point."

"Oh, I'm sorry girl. Well, anyway, I spent the night over at my male friend's house. He has a house over in the Villages of West Clay. When I was leaving this morning, I saw Tony standing on a porch across the street at one of the townhomes."

I started to get nervous. When Stacey first called me, I thought that maybe she was playing

162

around. It didn't appear to be that way anymore. Stacey was serious. She would never carry a joke this far. I continued to probe her for more information.

"Did you get a good look at him?"

"I sure did. He had on brown pants, brown shoes, and a brown shirt with stripes. He was also carrying what looked like a beige sweater in his hand."

My stomach immediately started to turn. My throat was dry and tight. I could not believe what Stacey was telling me. She described what Tony had on right down to the very same sweater that he was carrying in his hand when he walked into our apartment. Why would Tony lie about where he was last night? Why would Jay lie for him? There had to be a good reason for the lies. Maybe it wasn't a lie. Maybe Jay did move without my knowledge of the event. There had to be a good explanation for all of this.

"Are you okay, Karen?"

"Yes. I'm fine. I'm sure that there is a reason for all of the confusion. Maybe Tony and Jay stayed over at another one of their buddy's house or something."

"Karen, there's more. Jay wasn't with Tony. There was a woman standing on the porch with him. They were the only two people out there this morning. Tony and this woman walked out onto the porch from inside the townhome. They gave each other a hug, and then Tony got into his car and left."

My heart was pounding. My chest was tight. My breathing was shallow. What was happening? Was Tony with another woman last night? Did he spend the night with her? How could he do this to me? Why would he do this to me? My mind was flooded with questions.

"Did you recognize the woman on the porch?"

"She looked familiar to me, but I didn't know who she was. I asked my male friend if he knew her."

"What did he say?"

"He told me that it is her townhome. He said that she just moved there a few months ago. She just moved back to Indianapolis from Texas. He said her name is Laura."

"Laura?"

"Yep, Laura."

"That's the same name of Tony's ex-girlfriend."

"Really? Oh my God. Do you think that it was her?"

"I'm sure that it was."

"Are you going to say anything?"

"I don't know. I'm going to give you a call later, okay?"

"Sure. Are you sure that you are alright? You call me if you need anything. All that I need is a few minutes. I can slip on my sweatpants and head over to your apartment so that we can both give him an old-fashioned Indiana beat-down."

"I'm alright. I'll call you later."

When I got off the phone with Stacey, I didn't know what to do. I was hurt and confused. Half of me wanted to give Tony a chance to tell his side of the story. The other half wanted to take a butcher's knife out of our kitchen and gut him like a fish. How could Tony cheat on me? Was this the first time he had cheated on me, or had he done this before? How many times had he slept with Laura without my knowing? How long had this been going on behind my back?

There were so many questions that had to be answered. I fought to hold back my tears. My body became limp. My legs were no longer able to support me. I quickly sat down at the two-seater kitchen table in our kitchen area. I ran my sweaty hands through my sleep-matted hair. I then hobbled to the hallway bathroom, and I closed the door behind me. I fell to my knees, and I grabbed a hold of the toilet with both hands. It was then that I released last night's dinner and drinks. With every muscle spasm in my stomach, I could feel the regurgitation of not only the food and drinks that I had last night, but of my relationship and engagement. Each vomit weakened me more than the previous. I was drained.

After every ounce of food and liquid in my stomach was freed, I just sat on the floor with my back against the wall. I pulled both my knees to my chest, and I rested my forehead against my knees. What was I supposed to do? Was this the end of us? Should I bring it up to Tony and risk a huge argument and breakup? Maybe this was a one-time thing and Tony wouldn't let it happen again. Was Tony planning on leaving me? I didn't want to break up with Tony. I loved him very much. I also didn't want to be a fool. I didn't want a man that was a cheater. If Tony was in love with me, then why would he cheat on me? Was he still in love with Laura? I didn't know if I could forgive him. I didn't know if I should.

I always thought that all men cheated at some point, but not my man. I always thought that Tony was different from all the other cheating men out there. Tony knew of the bad relationships that I'd had. He had even helped me get over one. How could he do this to me, knowing how hurt I'd been before? Maybe I was jumping to conclusions. I was sure that Tony had an explanation for all of this. What explanation could he have? He was busted. My girl saw him in plain view coming out of another woman's home this morning.

I walked out of the bathroom weak and confused. I tried to hide the pain that I was feeling inside. I tried to hide the tears that I was holding back. I ignored the foul taste that was left in my mouth from my vomiting. I hesitantly searched for Tony. When I entered the bedroom, Tony was coming out of the master bathroom with a towel wrapped around his waist. He was using another smaller towel to dry the water out of his ears. I just stared at him until he noticed me.

"Oh. Hey, babe. What's going on?"

"Nothing. How was your night?"

"It was alright, aside from my passing out at Jay's."

I tried to hide my anger. That bastard lied to me in my face. He looked me directly in my eyes and spit out a lie like I was nothing to him. The voice in my head was telling me to claw his eyeballs out. I ignored that voice, and I continued to talk to my dishonest man.

"So, how is Jay doing these days?"

"Jay is doing alright. He still thinks that he can outsell me on the lot. So, other than being a little delusional, I'd guess that he's fine."

"Where did you guys end up going last night?"

"We went to the bowling alley for a few hours, and then we came back to Jay's apartment."

"The bowling alley? You were a little clean to go bowling, weren't you?"

"Well, we were planning on going to a night-club, but things didn't work out. We just decided to go to the bowling alley and play a few games and have some drinks."

That cheating ass did it again. He told another lie to my face. I knew Tony like no one else. There was no way that he was going to waste an outfit like that at the bowling alley. He had to be crazy to think that his lie would convince me. That was the sorriest lie that I had ever heard. It probably took both Tony and Jay all night to think of that sorry fairy tale.

"That's good that you and Jay were able to hang out last night. Does he still live on the west side of town?"

"He sure does. He lives in the same apartment that he has been living in for years. He's too cheap to move anywhere else. What about you? How was your night?"

"It was fine."

I stood there for a few seconds to see if there was anything else that Tony wanted to add. Maybe he forgot that he'd spent the night with his ex-girlfriend and not with Jay. I could tell that Tony was a little nervous during our conversation. As we were talking, he fumbled around on the bathroom countertops. Every time that he tried to pick something up, he'd knock something else over. He even put on my deodorant thinking that it was his. Something was obviously on his mind. It was the same lie that was on my mind.

I decided not to tell Tony what I knew. I don't know why. Maybe it was because I didn't want to leave Tony. I didn't want to deal with the issues that were brought up with those types of situations. I didn't want to argue about it. Most of all, I didn't want to hear him lie to me again. What if, for some strange reason, it wasn't Tony? Then he would think that I didn't trust him.

25 Tyson

I woke up this morning to the smell of coffee and breakfast coming from the kitchen of my loft. The sun was beaming through the mini blinds of my bedroom. I looked over at the other side of my bed and noticed the empty space. I staggered to the bathroom to empty my bladder. Soon after that, I headed downstairs to the kitchen. Joan was already fully dressed and preparing our places at the table. She had on a pair of low cut jeans and an IUPUI T-shirt. Joan smiled when she saw me walk into the kitchen.

"Hello, sir."

"Good morning, beautiful. How are you?"

"I'm doing fine this morning. How did you sleep?"

"I slept pretty well."

"That's good. I cooked us some breakfast. I can eat with you, and then I have to go to class."

I took a sip of the coffee that Joan had prepared for me. I then smiled at her, giving my approval. We both ate our portions of the breakfast that Joan made us, and then Joan hurried to collect her things so that she could leave. She grabbed the overnight bag that she brought over the previous night and headed for the door. Joan placed her hand on one side of my face, and she kissed the other side. She then smiled at me and kissed my lips. As I looked into Joan's beautifully slanted eyes, I could tell that she didn't really want to leave.

"You have a good day at school. Maybe you can meet me here again tonight after I get out of work."

"I would love to. Just call me and let me know what time."

"I will."

"Bye."

"Bye."

I finished my cup of coffee and started to get ready for work. I had a big week ahead of me. I told Joan this earlier in the weekend. That's probably why she fixed me breakfast this morning. She knew how important this week was to me. My team and I were nearing the completion of the Weber account at the firm. We were set for a meeting with the big managers and the Weber executives on Wednesday.

I arrived at work a little earlier than usual. I wanted to get a good jump on the things that I had to get done. Shortly after I had arrived at my desk,

Karen appeared with some documents for us to go over. She didn't seem like herself. She was still looking good as usual, but I could tell that she had something on her mind.

"Is everything alright?"

"Yes. Everything is fine. I'm just a little tired. I didn't get much sleep over the weekend."

"Worried about the Weber account?"

"Yes. I guess you can call it that."

"Well, I need you to recover very quickly. We both need to be one hundred percent today. We have a long day ahead of us."

"I know. I'll be fine."

Karen and I called a quick meeting with the rest of our team members to set the expectations for the day. We really wanted to complete the Weber account today. There were just a few things that needed to be finalized. After the meeting with our team, Karen sat with our web designer to approve the final touches to the proposed Weber website that we'd created. I viewed all of the television commercial skits that we'd created as well as all of the billboard design information.

All day long, my manager checked in on me to see if we were going to complete everything on schedule. I tried to avoid him the best that I could all day. The last thing that I needed was added stress. I knew just how important this account was to my company. Most of all, I knew how important it was for the advancement of my career. Having this account in my portfolio would be good leverage for promotional requests. This was the biggest account that I had ever worked on for my firm. We had worked with bigger companies before, but not with the amount of money that was invested by this client.

I was eyeball deep in documents and procedures all day. I saw Karen only once, although we talked to each other via cell phone on various occasions throughout the morning. We were both working very hard to get things done. My cell phone was ringing off the hook. I couldn't extinguish the fires fast enough. As soon as I would address a concern, another one would appear. I called Joan and told her that it was going to be a long night at work and that we would probably have to get together tomorrow instead. She understood my situation.

I walked by Karen's desk around six in the evening. She was checking some e-mails. Her hair was pulled into a ponytail. A few stray strands of her long hair draped both temples. Karen looked like I felt: tired and worn out from the day's events.

"Hey Karen, how's it going?"

Karen looked up at me. I could tell that she didn't even notice my standing there until I spoke to her.

"Oh. Hello, Tyson. Everything is everything. I have been going nonstop. I'm sure that your day has been somewhat identical to mine."

"You can say that again. It is already six o' clock, and you and I still have to go over our Power-Point presentation for Wednesday."

"I was just about to send you an e-mail to see when would be a good time to start on that."

"I am going to need about another hour or two to finalize some things, and then I'll be ready to start."

"Sounds good. I've already prepared myself for a long night."

After I left Karen's desk, I went to the vending machine and got a couple of packages of plain M&M's and two Cokes. I made my way back to Karen's desk and took a seat in one of the available chairs next to her desk.

"What are you doing?"

"I figured that if you have been working just as hard as I have been working today, you may have forgotten to eat lunch. So, with that in mind, I went and got us a little something to put in our stomachs and a little caffeine to give us a boost."

174

"Thank you, Tyson. That was sweet. Your assumption was correct. I did forget to eat lunch today."

"Well, I say that we both take a twenty-minute time-out and refuel our bodies and clear our minds."

"Amen to that."

Karen logged out of her e-mail account and turned her chair to face me. We both ate our packages of M&M's and sipped on our Cokes. I ate my M&M's one at a time to make them last longer. Karen ate hers a handful at a time. We joked a little and talked a little. She still was not herself. I knew that something was wrong with her, but I didn't press the issue. I was actually concerned about her. It didn't make me feel good to know that something was bothering her.

26 Karen

I tried to make it through the day without thinking about what Stacey told me. Every time that the thought of what Tony did to me and our relationship entered my mind, I would try to block it out. It wasn't hard for me to stay busy today with our deadline looming. This helped with my attempt to not think about my troubles at home.

Tyson and I spent hours putting our presentation together. We had lots of information that had to be implemented. Everyone else on our team had gone home for the day. As a matter of fact, the whole building was gone for the day. It was about ten o' clock, and my mind was overwhelmed. Although we were both very tired and worn out, we were pleased at what we had accomplished. Other than a few more needed add-ons, the presentation was complete.

It felt as if a huge weight had been lifted from my shoulders. I had been working very hard on this account, and to see it finally coming to a close was refreshing. Tyson looked drained. Earlier, he had taken off his suit jacket and rolled the sleeves of his white dress shirt halfway up his forearms. Tyson's solid black tie was loosened, and the top button of his shirt was unbuttoned. He sat down in the chair next to me.

"Well, it looks like we have done all that we can do today. I think that we should call it a night."

"I agree. We can go over the finishing touches with the rest of the team in the morning."

We both started to collect our personal effects. Tyson grabbed his black suit jacket and his leather briefcase. I grabbed my purse and my laptop bag. Tyson held the door to the conference room open for me as I passed through the doorway. After I exited the conference room, Tyson turned off the lights and followed behind me as I walked to the elevators. While we were waiting on the elevator to make the trip from the lobby area to the fourth floor, Tyson struggled to put on his suit jacket. Once he managed to put the jacket on, I noticed that the collar of his jacket was not folded down correctly. I smiled and helped him straighten his collar.

"What's so funny?" Tyson asked.

"Nothing. I'm just so accustomed to seeing you look like you just stepped off the cover of *GQ* magazine, so it's amusing to see you looking anything but perfect."

"Oh. So we have jokes, do we? Well, Ms. Karen, you are not quite looking like the beautiful model as you normally do."

"Now you are exaggerating. I don't think that I ever look like a model. Those girls have the perfect everything. They have the perfect hair, the perfect face, and not to mention, the perfect bodies."

"Are you insane? If you ask me, you have all of those qualities that you just mentioned and more."

I smiled a blushing smile. The moment was kind of uncomfortable, but I enjoyed the compliment. I finished fixing Tyson's collar. As I began to turn away from Tyson, I felt his hand gently touch my waist. Tyson pulled me close to him. He looked at me with a gentle stare. I didn't pull back away from him. Tyson then took both of his hands and pulled the rubber band out of my hair to let my hair fall to my shoulders. He smiled and ran his fingers through my hair to straighten it. As his fingertips gently grazed my scalp, tingles ran down my spine. Tyson then pulled me closer to him as he stared into my eyes. I should have pulled away, but I didn't want to.

Tyson kissed me on my cheek. His lips felt soft as his mustache tickled my skin. I could vividly smell the Sean John cologne that he was wearing. The unforgiveable aroma sparked my senses. My mind was telling me to pull away while I still had an option. My

178

body was telling me to accept whatever he was offering. My mind and my body were involved in a virtual battle. This left my own lips confused, so when Tyson lowered his head to kiss me, I didn't stop him.

Tyson's lips first pecked mine as if to make sure that is was alright. He stared into my eyes as his lips pecked mine again. After receiving confirmation from my own lips as they puckered to return the peck, both of our mouths opened to receive the moment.

As I kissed Tyson, I wondered if the kiss that Tony shared with Laura was as electrifying as the one that I was sharing with Tyson. Did Tony enjoy his kiss as well as I was enjoying mine? Did he think about me while he was kissing Laura? As Tyson and I continued our kiss, my body was limp in his arms. The longer the kiss went on, the more involved I became. My mind and my body continued their virtual battle. Eventually my mind would get the upper hand. I was brought back to sanity with the ding from the elevator when it reached our floor. I pulled my lips away from his. I couldn't do it. I was not going to do Tony like he did me.

I wanted Tyson badly. My entire body did, but my mind would not let me dig a bigger hole.

"I can't do this. We shouldn't have done this. We work together. How could we…"

"I'm sorry. I didn't mean…"

"No. It wasn't all your fault. I am to blame as much as you are."

The look on Tyson's face was that of a little boy who just had his PlayStation taken away from him. Tyson stopped the elevator door from closing back. We both gathered our things that we let fall to the hallway floor during our moment of connection, and we entered the elevator. It was a long elevator ride down to the lobby on the first floor. Not a word was said. I couldn't believe that I had kissed him. What was I thinking? I glanced over at Tyson, and my lipstick was all over his lips. He was just standing there and staring at the elevator doors. We were both embarrassed at what just happened. I was too ashamed to look at my reflection in the mirrored ceiling of the elevator. I could still feel the tingle of his goatee on my chin. My lips were still wet with the saliva from another man. I sucked my bottom lip to taste the remains of his kiss. I closed my eyes in shame. My eyes opened when I heard the ding from the elevator again signaling that we had made it to our first-floor destination.

"Can you give me a ride to my car?" Tyson asked.

"Sure."

Tyson and I walked from the elevator to the front door of our office building without another word. We then exited the building and walked to the outside company parking lot, which was attached to one side of the building. This was the very lot that Tyson had given me his parking pass for. The lot was totally empty except for my car. My car was parked in the last parking space next to the gate that separated the parking lot from the alley. The front of my car was facing our office building. We walked across the entire lot without a single word. The walk across the parking lot was long and silent.

When we approached my car, I walked over to Tyson's side of the car to unlock the door. Under normal circumstances, I would have used my remote to unlock the doors, but the battery in the remote was dead. I had meant to replace it over the weekend, but I forgot. I unlocked the passenger side door and opened it. Tyson placed his briefcase on the floor inside the car and eased my laptop bag off my shoulders. He placed it on the floor with his briefcase. Then, he turned around and looked at me. He still didn't utter a word. Neither did I.

I used my thumb to gently wipe my lipstick off his lips. We both smiled at each other. I spoke very soft and low.

"Tyson, I have a fiancé. We shouldn't be doing things like that. I can't deny that I am attracted to you, but it's still not right."

"I know. I have a girlfriend also. I don't think that she would approve either."

I had never heard Tyson mention a girlfriend before. I knew that he was dealing with lots of females, but I never heard him actually claim one before. This did something to me. I actually felt jealous. I was jealous that someone in fact earned the title of "girlfriend" from Tyson. My mind and my body repeated their virtual fight. But my mind was not the stronger one anymore. My body was beating my mind to a bloody pulp.

I kissed Tyson. We continued our moment. As I kissed him, I placed both of my hands inside his suit jacket, and I let them explore his back and his chest. I began to kiss his neck as I unbuttoned his shirt. I could feel his breath on my ears. He was breathing heavily as my wet lips kissed his chest. Tyson grabbed my hair and pulled my face to his. He kissed me with such tenderness. My body became limp in his arms again. Tyson grabbed me by the back of my thighs and lifted me into the air, not missing a single beat with his wanting kisses. I wrapped my legs around his waist. Tyson walked around to the back of my car and sat me on the trunk. He opened my ruffled blouse and lifted my push-up bra to let my breasts fall.

Tyson gave my breasts the attention that they had been lacking. His mouth was warm, and his kisses were wet. I then reached into my purse, which was still on my shoulder, and I pulled out a condom. I placed it into Tyson's palm as he kissed my belly. He paused and looked up at me. Our eyes met for a few seconds, and then Tyson helped me down off the trunk of the car. We kissed a little more, and then he started to unbuckle my studded belt. Tyson then unbuttoned the two buttons on my plaid, wide-legged pants. Tyson turned me around, and I let the front of my body fall onto the trunk of my car. After a few seconds my pants fell past my brown Nine West pumps and onto the concrete. Shortly after that, my low-rise thong followed the same path. Tyson began to kiss my back. I could feel him enter me as I closed my eyes and exhaled. I exhaled all of the stress that the day had caused. I exhaled the feeling of betrayal that I had from what I knew about Tony. I exhaled all of the sexual frustration that I'd had with Tyson. I exhaled and exhaled.

With every motion, I could feel the cold steel from the rear fender of my car on my chest and stomach. I stretched out both of my arms, and the palms of my hands were flat on the trunk lid. I don't think that

General Motors had this in mind when they designed the car. I looked up at the downtown buildings and the empty sidewalks as Tyson and I continued our flesh-satisfying act. A few cars drove by, ignorant to what was happening in the dark corner of that parking lot. Tyson then turned me around and kissed me again. He opened the back door of my car, and I eased in and onto my back. My knees parted to signal an invitation. Tyson accepted without hesitation. We went on for another ten minutes, and then we were done. The back door of my car was open the entire time and Tyson's legs were hanging outside of the car. Satisfaction and guilt both filled the backseat. The courtesy light on the ceiling of my car was shining in my eyes and Tyson's head was against my cheek.

We both searched for our discarded clothing in the dark of the parking lot. After getting dressed the best that we could, I drove Tyson to the garage where his car was. Before he got out of my car, he leaned over and we shared another kiss. Tyson exited the car and disappeared through the entrance doors of the parking garage.

During my drive home, my mind was all over the place. What just happened? Why did I let it happen? I wondered if I had performed the act out of revenge or for my own satisfaction. Maybe it was both.

184

I started to feel guilty. Regardless of what Tony did to me, I was responsible for my own actions. I was the one who had to look myself in the mirror every day. How could I go to work tomorrow and look Tyson in the face? How could I go home tonight with a wet thong and look my fiancé in the face? This was the most important week of my life, and I was tainting it with one of the most terrible things that I had ever done. I didn't even know if Tony really cheated on me or not. I wondered if I would have let this happen if Stacey had never told me the news about Tony.

I almost let all of my judgment and fears drown out the fact that I had liked it. The moment that I shared with Tyson was amazing. I had never felt passion like that before. I felt as if I was irresistible, and Tyson had to have me right there. That moment made me feel sexy. It was almost as if I had become another person. If I were watching it on television, then I would want to be that girl on the trunk of the car. The only downfall was that it could not continue. I could not continue to cheat on Tony. I loved him too much. Most of all, I could never let Tony find out about it. There was no way that he would forgive me for it, regardless of what he had already done. Tony already had his suspicions of Tyson and me in the past, and his finding out about this would confirm his suspicions.

I was in a lonely place. I had a huge secret that I couldn't tell anyone, not even Stacey. I cheated on my fiancé in what appeared to be revenge without knowing for sure if Tony had actually cheated on me. I was driving home to my fiancé with a warm feeling supplied by someone else. My mouth had the aftertaste of someone else's kiss. My thong covered a damp place that was sore from someone else's performance.

I pulled over at the entrance of my apartment complex. I adjusted my clothing and reapplied my makeup in the rear-view mirror. I located some perfume that I had in my purse, and I sprayed it over my clothing to hide Tyson's smell.

27 Tony

I heard the door to our apartment open and close at a little before midnight. I was in the bed, but I was not asleep. I was watching SportsCenter on television when Karen entered our bedroom.

"Long day?"

"Yes it was, but we were able to complete the work for the big account that we've been working on. We are going to present it on Wednesday."

"Congratulations. I figured that you'd had a long day, but you could have called to let me know what was going on."

"You're right. I'm so sorry. I just got caught up in my work."

"Understood."

I was very disturbed that Karen came home so late. What is it that she has to do at work until almost midnight? I tried to hide my anger. I would not have been so upset if she would have called me to let me know. Karen started to take off her earrings and her other jewelry when her cell phone rang. I already knew who it was. Karen answered her BlackBerry and informed the person on the phone that she had made it home alright. She made sure to make the call short and simple.

"So, who was that?"

"Oh, it was just Tyson calling to make sure that I made it home safely."

"Tyson, huh? So, does he call all of the other team members to make sure that they get home safely, too?"

"I don't know. I never ask. Besides, only Tyson and I were working late tonight."

"Why are you two the only ones that work late? What happened to the rest of your team?"

"Tyson and I are the ones who are mainly in charge of this project. We have the biggest bulk of the work that is needed to complete the account."

As we talked, I could feel myself beginning to anger even more. I was really annoyed at the situation. Something just was not right. I thought the purpose of having a team was to share the workload.

Karen had been coming home late consistently for the past month. Every time that I asked her about it, she told me that she and Tyson had things to take care of. I never heard her talk about her other team members. I didn't even know their names.

"Are you and Tyson messing around?"

"What? How could you ask me something like that?"

"I don't know, but I just did. So, answer the question."

"You know, you've got some nerve to ask me something like that."

"You still have not answered the question."

"No! Tyson and I are not messing around. Are you happy with your answer?"

I knew that Karen wouldn't appreciate my asking her that question, but I had to know. I could see the frustration in Karen's face as we had the conversation. I could also feel my own blood starting to boil.

"So, if I were to call Tyson and ask him, would he say the same?"

At that moment, I reached for Karen's cell phone. Karen snatched the cell phone off the dresser before I could reach it.

"What is wrong with you? Why are you acting crazy?"

"You said that you and Tyson aren't messing around, so I just want to call him and see what he has to say about it. If he is a real man, then he wouldn't lie to me. If he does lie to me, then I will just have to beat him like a stepchild."

"You will not touch him! Tyson hasn't done anything to you."

"Are you taking up for him? Oh, I guess that you feel as though it is your job to protect him. The both of you are around each other all day and late into the night. When you aren't around each other, you talk on the phone constantly. Then, to make things worse than that, he calls you at midnight to make sure that you are alright. That's my job! Not his!"

I was really angry. How could she defend another man? I was supposed to be the main person in her life, not Tyson. Lately, she had spent more time with Tyson than she had with me. My mind started to drift. I began to think about the canceled lunches and dates. I began to think about the lonely nights that I ate pizza all alone. I remembered all the times that I tried to call her and was sent straight to her voicemail. I don't know what came over me. At that very moment, I grabbed Karen's left hand, and I repossessed the engagement ring that I gave her.

Time froze. There was a dead silence in our world. Karen looked at me as her eyes saturated with tears. She had a look of shock on her face. Her mouth hung open in disbelief. I was shocked myself. I couldn't believe what I had just done. It was like an outer-body experience. My reflexes had accomplished a task that my mind did not approve. Taking that ring off Karen's finger was like unplugging a lamp without turning it off first. There was an instant discon-

190

nect between us. You could almost feel the energy leaving the room as the ring was removed from her finger. Karen looked down at the smooth spot on her finger that once housed her engagement ring. It was pale from the lack of sun. She looked at it as if she had never seen it without that ring on it.

"So, it's like that, huh? Are you saying that you don't trust me? After all that I have gone through for you? You have a lot of nerve."

Karen started shaking her head back and forth as if she didn't believe the events that were taking place. She then started to laugh to herself. It was almost disturbing to witness. Karen's lips smiled in one corner as she laughed to herself. It was a devilish type of smile. She wiped away some of the tears on her cheek with her palms. Her chest swelled as if she had found a new breath of strength.

"You of all people should be the last person accusing someone of being unfaithful."

"What is that supposed to mean?"

"Don't stand there and act innocent. Have you been doing anything lately that I should be concerned about?"

"What are you talking about?"

"I'm talking about Laura, Tony!"

My heart stopped. My stomach began to turn, and my testicles ran to hide from her. She knew about

Laura. How could this be? The tears started flowing out of Karen's eyes like water from a kitchen faucet. That new breath of strength that she had found earlier in the conversation was gone. I could easily interpret the hurt and anger in Karen's face.

"I know about Laura, Tony. Stacey saw you coming out of her townhome that morning when you were supposed to be at Jay's. She described what you had on all the way down to the sweater that you were carrying, so please don't try to lie about it. I was on the phone with her when you came home that morning. You lied to my face when I asked you about your night. You looked me straight in the eyes and lied like I meant nothing to you. So, please just tell me the truth."

I was shocked. I had actually forgotten how to talk. I had lost all memory of how to form a word. My mind was vacant. I didn't know vowels, nouns, adjectives, or anything else that I had learned in elementary school.

"Aren't you going to say anything?"

"What do you want me to say?"

"The truth. I want the truth, Tony. Was it you?"

I wanted to answer, but I couldn't. I tried to talk, but my mouth would not move. I was terrified. I was terrified at the thought of Karen's hating me.

192

"Answer me, Tony. Was it you?"

"Yes. Yes, it was me."

"You bastard!"

After my answer, Karen broke down. She was crying uncontrollably. I tried to hold her, but she wouldn't let me touch her.

"Karen, I spent the night over there, but we didn't do anything."

"What kind of fool do you think I am? If you think that I am going to believe that you spent the night over your ex-girlfriend's house and nothing happened, then you must be out of your rabbit mind."

"Karen, I know that it sounds crazy, but I didn't touch her."

"Why do you continue to lie to me as if I am some tramp that you just met in a bar? Do I mean anything to you? Do you even have an ounce of respect for me?"

The tears continued to flow. Karen's face was red from the pain. It hurt me to see her like that. There was no way that she was going to believe me. If someone told me the exact story, I wouldn't believe it either. I wasn't completely innocent, though. I didn't have any business being at Laura's townhome in the first place. Even though Laura and I didn't do anything, I should not have been there.

"Karen, you have to believe me. We didn't do anything."

"Tony, please stop the lies. I can't take them anymore. You have to tell me the truth. Even if by some crazy likelihood the two of you did not have sex, you cannot stand there and tell me that you didn't at least kiss her."

"No. I did not. I admit that I was there, but I didn't kiss her, and most of all I did not have sex with her."

"Why are you doing this to me? If you love me at all, then just tell me the truth."

I could see the pain in Karen's face. She continued to cry as she covered her face with her hands. Karen was pleading for the truth. It was like she wanted me to say that I had sex with Laura. It was like Karen was begging me to tell her that Laura and I kissed. I didn't think she would accept any other information. Her mind was already made up about us. I couldn't take seeing Karen like that. She was hurt. It hurt me to see the pain that she was feeling. I had never seen Karen like that. I wanted to stop the pain.

"Ok. I did. Laura and I had sex."

Karen pulled her hands from her face. Her makeup was mixed with her tears. She looked up at me with an empty gaze. Karen's chest was rising and falling as her heart was breaking inside of it. I told her what she wanted to hear. It wasn't true, but it was what she wanted to hear. Laura and I did not have sex that night or any other night since she had moved back to Indianapolis. I hadn't even kissed her. The most that we had done is share a few hugs, but that was all. After I confessed to an act that I didn't actually commit, regret consumed my body.

I had to say it. If I didn't tell Karen that Laura and I had sex, then she would have thought that I didn't care about her. In her mind, I was lying to her. The last thing that I wanted to do was to have Karen thinking that I didn't love her. I loved her with all of my heart. I respected her and would do anything for her. I wanted her to know that.

"I messed up. I know that, but we can work through this. I don't want to lose you over this."

"Were you thinking like that before or after you were on top of her?"

"I guess that I wasn't doing much thinking. That's why we are both standing here now. Please forgive me."

"I can't. I can't forgive you. There is no way that we can move on. You gambled. You gambled our trust and our relationship. The bad thing about gambling is that there is a chance that you will lose. You lost me."

"Karen, I'm sorry."

"Are you sorry that you cheated on me, or are you just sorry that you got caught? How could you do that to me? I can't forgive you, Tony. I want to, but I can't. I don't like all of the lies that you have told me. I don't like the person that I have become because of you. Your actions have made me weak and insecure during a time when I need to be at my best. I don't like how this feels. I don't want to feel like this. I don't like how I've been acting because of you."

I tried to give Karen the ring back, but she refused it. I tried to take hold of her hand, and she pulled it back. I knew that admitting to something that didn't happen was dumb, but I had my reasons. I'd met Laura on numerous occasions for lunch without Karen's knowing about it. We'd had several phone conversations, not to mention the date we went on that night. That was cheating in itself. I had cheated in my mind. In my mind, I wanted Laura. I daydreamed of kissing her and making love to her. I wondered what it would be like to hold her in my arms again. My mouth watered for Laura. I compared Laura and Karen on a daily basis. I told Laura my troubles and my feelings. Those were things that should have been shared only with Karen. I permitted Laura back into my life. If Laura did ever try to make a move on me, I'm not sure that I would have refused her. I'm not sure that I would want to.

196

After hours of uncomfortable conversation, I took my earned spot on the couch. The entire apartment was dark. Thoughts ran through my mind like a river. I didn't know what I was going to do. I didn't know where I was going to go. It was too late to figure all of that out. I was exhausted. I was facing the thought of losing Karen. There was no way that she would let me continue to live in the apartment with her while we were at odds. My life was at a halt. Karen was right. I did gamble our relationship.

My eyes started to water, and my nose became stuffy. I didn't want to lose Karen. I was mad at myself for letting Laura back into my life. I should not have taken Laura's phone number that night at the bar. I should never have called her. Karen was the best thing that had ever happened to me, and I was on the verge of losing her over an ex-girlfriend that left me several years ago.

After about twenty minutes on the couch, I heard footsteps walking toward me. I noticed Karen's frame in the darkness of the room. She didn't say a word. She sat on the couch, and then she laid her head deep into my chest. My shirt became damp from her tears. I rubbed her back with one hand while I wiped my own tears with the other. Not a word was spoken. My lady and I cried together. I wondered if she was having the same thoughts that I was. I felt

197

lost. I felt lonely and confused. I didn't know what was next. I didn't know if I should fight to get Karen back or go away peacefully.

28 Tony

"You did what? What is wrong with you?"

Jay was standing over me. He had both his arms stretched out to the heavens for an answer. I was sitting on his couch with my bags at my feet. I had just told Jay about the previous night's drama.

"I know that it sounds crazy."

"Crazy? Crazy is a compliment for what you did. Stupid is a better word for it. What in the world would possess you to tell your fiancé that you slept with another woman? You didn't even sleep with Laura."

"Jay, don't you think that I know that?"

"I'm just saying, you should have at least gotten some kind of satisfaction out of it. Did you at least get some *for the good times* sex from Karen last night?"

"No, I didn't even try. That was the last thing that was on my mind last night."

"No, the last thing on your mind should have been telling her that you slept with your ex. That was really dumb. You have done a lot of dumb things in the past, but I think this one wins you the gold medal in the not-so-smart Olympics."

I knew that Jay would give me a hard time. I called him in the morning and asked him if I could stay over at his place for a few days until I figured out what I was going to do. I was almost too embarrassed to call him. When I got up this morning, Karen had already left for work. I had the day off, and Jay didn't have to be at work until one.

After Jay left for work, I sat on his couch and tried to clear my thoughts. I was worn out from the night before. I didn't have a clue as to what I should do. Every time that my mind focused on Karen, I found myself fighting back tears. I couldn't think straight. I was a wreck. I lost my girl, my apartment, and my mind in the same night. I felt like a man without a country. I never realized how much I cared for Karen until last night. Don't get me wrong. I always knew that I was in love with Karen, but I didn't have a gauge of how much until last night. I sacrificed our relationship for her feelings. I gave up everything just to stop the hurt that she was feeling.

I have to confess that telling Karen that I slept with Laura was dumb. The bad thing about it was that I couldn't take it back. I had already crossed the line. There was no way that I could go back to Karen and tell her that I didn't sleep with Laura. Karen would never believe me. She would probably call the mental ward to come and pick me up.

I couldn't help but wonder whether I should try to fix things with Karen or rekindle things with Laura. There was an obvious attraction between me and Laura. My mind continued to compare the two. It was clear that I still had a physical draw to Laura, but was it love? I had spent a surplus of time with her lately, and we had really connected. At one time, Laura was my world. I was very much in love with her. I was unable to imagine myself being in love with anyone else until she left and Karen came along. Was Karen a rebound? I wouldn't dare to question whether or not I was in love with Karen. The way that I felt at that very moment was evidence of the fact.

Karen was the woman whom I'd asked to marry me. We were engaged to be married. The ring that I still had five years of payments left on was now in my pocket surrounded by snot tissue. The question still remained: Should I try to get her back? I could probably make things right again between us if I really put forth the effort. It would take a long time to regain her trust, but it would be worth it. With all of that said, Karen would still have to agree to take me back. She would have to forgive me and accept her ring back. Doubt rushed into my mind. For years I had planned my entire future around our being together for the rest of our lives. Every goal that I had made included Karen.

On the other hand, those same goals that I had planned for me and Karen were once planned for me and Laura. If Laura never left me in the first place, Karen and I may have never even dated.

My mind continued to sway back and forth between the two. I felt like a madman. Was I in love with two women? How did I get myself into this predicament? What was I thinking? I should have never accepted Laura's phone number that night, but if I didn't accept it, then I would have been ignoring the true feelings that I had buried inside of me. All of the thinking and questions supplied my brain with a massive headache.

I walked to Jay's bathroom, and I opened the medicine cabinet. I scanned through its contents, searching for Tylenol or Excedrin. My eyes narrowed as my headache intensified. While I scanned the contents inside of Jay's medicine cabinet, I noticed a few disturbing items. I saw pimple creams, condoms, intimacy lubrication, female condoms, male enhancement pills, and even a bottle of douche. At that moment, I came to the realization that my best friend was a freak. I laughed internally and shook my head as I walked from Jay's bathroom to the kitchen to get a glass of water for my headache treatment.

Once I made it to the kitchen, I grabbed a White Castle cup out of Jay's upper cabinet, and I filled it with water from the kitchen faucet. I tossed two of the Excedrin pills into my mouth, and then I flushed them down with water. After that, I just leaned against the counter for a while. I would shake my head every time that I thought about the mess that I had created. It all felt like a bad dream.

I walked back into the living room, and I sat on the couch. I took my cell phone out of my pocket, and I dialed Karen's number. She didn't answer. I left her a message: *"Karen, this is Tony. Please call me. I really would like to talk to you."*

Afterward, Karen's voicemail gave me the option to review my message, delete it, or finalize it. I reviewed the message. I sounded so weak. I sounded desperate. It sounded like I was crazy. It actually sounded exactly how I was feeling at the time. After reviewing the message, I decided to delete it. Her voicemail gave me the option to re-record another message, so I did. I went through this scenario with her voicemail ten times. Every time that I recorded a new message, it sounded worse than the previous. I eventually approved and finalized one of my messages to be sent to her voicemail.

I turned on Jay's television to try to take my mind off things. I turned to one of the local affiliate stations. Judge Karen's courtroom show was on. Of course this show would be on when I was trying not to think about Karen. I continued to change the channels with the Comcast remote control. I turned to BET. Every video that came on reminded me of Karen. I heard and witnessed things within the videos that had never stood out to me before. Then, after one of the videos ended, Rocsi and Terrence, the video hosts of *106 & Park*, appeared on the television. Rocsi and Karen had similar features. This started to remind me of Karen once again. I fought back the tears. Frustrated, I just turned off the television.

I tried to listen to the radio to take my mind off things, but that didn't work either. I was listening to the *Russ Parr Morning Show*, and his co-host Alfredas was reading the horoscopes. Her voice was similar to Laura's voice. Then, the vision of Laura danced around inside my head. I quickly turned the radio station to the *Tom Joyner Morning Show*.

Tom and J. Anthony Brown were laughing and joking about players getting caught. It was very funny, but I had to turn off the radio.

I grabbed my cell phone from my pocket again, but this time I dialed Laura's number. But I didn't press the talk button to make the call. I called Karen's phone again, and she didn't answer. I left her another voicemail message. Of course, I called her phone

204

about twenty different times throughout the day without any success. It was obvious that Karen didn't have anything to say to me. I finally fell asleep on Jay's couch to the sound of silence and feeling of loneliness. I never would have imagined that the silence would be so loud.

29 Tyson

I opened my eyes and I immediately saw Joan sitting on the edge of my bed. She was staring at me while I was sleeping.

"Good morning."

"Good morning. What time is it?"

"It's a little after seven. I have to head to campus to work on some projects for class."

Joan was fully dressed. She was looking really good. Her natural locks were pulled into a ponytail, and she had on a blue Chicago Cubs baseball cap. Joan was wearing a pair of skinny jeans and a blue T-shirt that matched her hat. Her smile was as bright as ever. Joan kissed me on my forehead before standing to her feet.

"Are you going to walk me out?"

"Sure."

I rose from my resting position and maneuvered my way out of the tangled covers that were on my bed. I then followed Joan down the cold, iron staircase to the main floor. Joan grabbed her distressed-leather book bag off the sofa, and she headed for the door. She softly kissed me on my lips before she left. I admired her frame as she walked down the green carpeted hallway of my building in the direction of the elevators. I watched her step inside the elevator before I closed the door to my loft. I walked into the kitchen, and I opened the refrigerator. A few moments went by, and then I closed the stainless steel door of the refrigerator without taking anything out of it. I made my way back up the cold, iron staircase to the bedroom level of the loft. Once upstairs, I went into the bathroom to relieve myself of all the bodily fluids that had built up over the night. I must have stood over that toilet for about five minutes. It sounded like someone was pouring an entire pitcher of water into the toilet. The yellowish color of my urine was a sign to me that I needed to drink more water throughout the day.

After I unloaded my bladder, I washed my hands and began to brush my teeth. I used my reflection in the mirror to examine my smile. I then dropped my red and black boxers, and I opened the frameless glass door of the shower stall. Once inside, I turned the venetian-bronze handle of the shower's faucet. The first burst of water from the shower head was extremely cold. I jumped as soon as the cold water touched me. After a few seconds, the water turned warm. I closed my eyes as the water from the shower head soaked my face and my scalp. As I showered, my mind focused on the important meeting that I was in for. It was the big day. We had to convene with the Weber executives to present our work. Although my company was under contract with Weber, they still had an opportunity to pull out of the arrangement if they were not pleased with our efforts and what we had to offer them. I went over my presentation in my mind over a thousand times. I was preparing for one of the most significant meetings of my professional career. To say that I was nervous would be an under-statement. Of course, I was prepared to hide my anxi-ety during the meeting.

After my shower, I stepped out of the stall onto the cold ceramic-tiled floor. As I dried off with my bath towel, the house phone started to ring. It wasn't the normal ring that it does when someone calls me. It was the special ring that it does when someone calls from the intercom system in the entryway of my building. I hurried to get to the phone, but by the time I had reached it, the caller had hung up. I grabbed a pair of black boxers out of my top dresser drawer, and I slipped them on. I walked toward the bathroom again when I heard a tap on the front door. I figured that Joan may have forgotten to grab something on her way out this morning. I wondered why she didn't just call my cell phone and have me bring whatever it was by the university on my way to work.

I hurried down the cold, iron stairway and jogged across the hardwood flooring in my living room. I was almost out of breath when I made it to the front door. I turned the egg-shaped doorknob and started to open the door.

"Did you forget some…"

To my surprise it was Karen.

"Karen? What are you doing here?"

She didn't say a word. She immediately kissed me. Karen's hands searched my shoulder blades and the small of my back as she kissed me very sensually. I didn't pull away from her. She walked me further inside of my loft as she closed the door behind her. I opened the double-breasted, swing pea coat that Karen was wearing, and I let it fall to the hardwood flooring in my living room. We continued to kiss without any interruption. Her hands continued to stroke my back. My hands were busy unbuttoning Karen's long-sleeve, silk blouse. As soon as the black and white blouse was open, I allowed it to take its place on the hardwood flooring next to Karen's coat. I continued to walk backward as we kissed, until the backs of my legs touched the arm of my sofa. Karen continued to walk frontward as we kissed, and I fell backward over the arm of the sofa and onto the soft pillows. Karen was on top of me. Karen then began to kiss my neck and my chest. She never said a word to me.

She stood up and slipped out of her black, pleated skirt. She then reached both of her arms behind her back to open her bra. I just stared at her like a kid in line at the mall, waiting to sit on Santa's lap. My boxers did very little in hiding how I felt after I saw her exposed breasts. Karen then slipped out of her black thong and mounted her flawless, bare body on top of mine. I was really worked up. I kissed her even harder than before. I grabbed her shoulders, and I maneuvered myself to be on top of her. She was beautiful. I began to kiss her stomach. Karen squirmed and arched her back as my tongue danced around her navel. She tightly wrapped her legs around me. I continued to let my tongue taunt her.

I then turned Karen over on her stomach. She hid her face in the soft pillows of the sofa as she took hold of her long, black hair with both hands. I started to kiss the area between her shoulders. I allowed my tongue to outline the entire span of her spine. Karen moaned as I teased her. My hands caressed her arms as my lips explored her back. I then allowed my tongue to gently run over her backside and down to the back of her thighs. I gently sucked on the back of her thighs as I kissed them softly. Karen rose to her
210

elbows. Her eyes were closed as she pointed her chin toward the coffered ceiling of my loft. Her hair draped her shoulders. I gave equal attention to both of her thighs. I then tasted the back of Karen's knees, and I nibbled on her calves.

I noticed that Karen was still wearing her heels. I pulled her shoes off her feet, one foot at a time. Our last encounter was quick. I wanted this one to last. I wanted to enjoy every moment of it. After I dropped her shoes onto the floor, I then began to caress Karen's feet. I massaged her toes. I massaged the balls of her feet. I massaged her heels. Karen's feet were well manicured and soft. Her toenails were painted light pink. Her toes were slender and unblemished. I marveled at how pretty her feet were. Karen continued to moan as I placed her toes inside of my mouth. My tongue softly stroked the top of her toes as the bottom of her toes lightly grazed the roof of my mouth.

I enjoyed it just as much as Karen did. As I gave her toes some much-deserved attention, I permitted one of my hands to continue to massage her foot as the other caressed her calve. I also made sure to kiss Karen's ankles during my oral exploration of her body. The sun peered through the blinds as the morning matured. Karen then reached into her purse that was sitting on the floor next to the sofa. She grabbed a condom out of it. Karen then rose to her knees and turned around to face me. She motioned for me to sit on the sofa. I did as I was told. Karen stood over me and grabbed both sides of my boxers and pulled them off. She used her teeth to tear off a corner of the Trojan wrapper. She then freed the contents of the package. In a very sexy manner, Karen placed the condom on me. She then climbed on top of me and started to kiss me again. We kissed for several minutes before we actually started intercourse. Once we started, it was amazing.

Karen grabbed the back of my head with both of her hands as she pressed her cheek into my neck. I could feel her breathing on my collarbone. With every move that Karen made, I could feel my neck getting warm from her heavy breathing. I closed my eyes and tried to concentrate to keep from ending things prematurely. Karen's soft hair draped over both of our faces as she worked. I inhaled the sweet and delicate scent of her mane. Karen's lustful breathing amplified in volume. She then started to kiss me again. Her mouth was cold and wet. Strands of her hair became intertwined within our sensual kiss.

I grabbed both of Karen's legs as I stood up from our location on the sofa. Karen's legs were still wrapped around my waist, and her arms held me close to her. I walked over to the dining room table and rested her on top of it. I then began to make my presence known. Karen leaned back and let her shoulders rest on the table. She grabbed two fistfuls of her hair as I wrote my chapter in her book of emotional ties. Karen whined as we continued to shatter the trust that both of our significant others had in us. She gripped the red linen placemats that were on the dining room table as her whimpers grew louder. Her breathing hurried as her back arched and she began to shake. I continued to work. Karen's shoulders rose and fell continuously onto the dining room table as I continued my work.

A few more minutes went by before my breathing started to match hers. I tried to hurry in a few more strokes before I reached my zenith. My body trembled as it collapsed on top of Karen. We were both breathing heavily. Karen's beautiful hair fixed to the sweat on her chest. I could feel her stomach rising and falling underneath mine. We kissed. This time the kisses were softer. I ran my fingers through her hair to remove the stray strands from her face. Karen looked up at me from her position on the table. Her face was flushed. Her breathing had not slowed down yet. Karen's face was damp with sweat. She raised one of her hands and placed it on the side of my face. She then used the same hand to wipe away the beads of sweat that were on my forehead.

30 Tyson

My morning commute to work was very interesting. My mind kept replaying this morning's encounter with Karen. It was all totally unexpected. After the morning's actions, Karen went to the half bathroom on the main floor of my loft to freshen up. I could hear the water from the bathroom faucet running as Karen washed away my scent and passionate kisses from her body. In my mind, I imagined seeing all of our secrets, sex, and lies swirling around in a water funnel as they were all forced down the granite sink's drain. After her quick cleansing, Karen got dressed and then she left my loft to go to work. After she left, I just sat on the sofa for a few minutes to gather my thoughts. I started to think about how lucky I was that Joan didn't walk in on us. I got so caught up in the moment that I wasn't thinking straight. If Joan would have walked in on us, it would have been the start of a hideous state of affairs. Before going back upstairs to freshen up, I rushed to straighten up the living room to hide any evidence of what took place. I used my hands to smooth out all of the knee and booty dents that were left on the seat cushions of the chocolate microfiber sofa. I re-aligned all of the sofa's sand-colored pillows to make them look like they were still on display in the window of the furniture store that I had purchased them from. I then did a thorough sweep of the living room to make sure that no other evidence was left at the scene of the crime. I even sprayed Lysol around the entire loft to make sure that it didn't smell like a woman had been in there.

After I took my second shower of the morning, I made my second attempt to get dressed. I removed the plastic covering off my black suit that I had picked up from the cleaners over the weekend. I then spent a few moments staring at my vast collection of neck ties, trying to determine which one was the right one to wear for the day. After selecting the red silk tie with black diagonal stripes, I grabbed one of my new white dress shirts that I had recently purchased, and I began to iron it. After I did my best to press out all of the creases that were made from the shirt being fold-ed inside the package, I finally got dressed.

I adjusted my tie as I walked down the iron staircase to the main level of my loft. As soon as the soles of my Steve Madden oxfords touched the hard-wood flooring of the main level, my front door opened and Joan walked in. My heart skipped a beat as my body refused to take another step. My eyes examined Joan's facial expression to make sure that everything was alright. I glanced at both of Joan's hands to make sure that she wasn't carrying any sharp objects or firearms. A bead of sweat ran down the side of my face. I wondered why Joan was back so soon. My voice lacked all of its base and puberty as I attempted to speak.

"Hey."

"Hey. I was hoping that you were still here. I wanted to bring you some breakfast before you headed off to work."

As Joan spoke, I noticed that she was carrying a paper bag with the McDonald's logo on it. I exhaled in relief. I smiled from ear to ear. I walked over to where Joan was standing, and I gave her a big hug. I inhaled deeply as I held her. Joan removed the Cubs baseball cap from her head and gave me a peck on my lips. Her smile mimicked mine. I stared at her as her smile lit the room. Joan escorted me over to the dining room table. My eyes opened wide as we walked closer to it. At that moment I realized I had forgotten to straighten the dining room table after my early morning episode with Karen. My heart began to race. I noticed the look on Joan's face as we approached the table.

"Why are all of the placemats scattered all over the table?"

"Oh. I was making some last minute changes to some documents this morning, and I forgot to clean up when I was done."

Joan believed my lie as she straightened the linen placemats. I took my place at the table as Joan emptied the contents of the McDonald's bag. She handed me a sausage breakfast burrito and a small orange juice. Joan claimed the seat next to mine.

"Did you get anything for yourself?"

"No. I stopped and grabbed a bite to eat after I left here this morning. I just figured that I would bring you something to eat before you leave for work. My next class isn't until ten."

Joan continued to talk to me. I didn't have any clue as to what she was talking about. I could not focus on our conversation. I tried not to make it obvious that I was looking around the dining area to make sure that I had not forgotten to remove or clean up anything else. Once I saw that the coast was clear, I felt reassured. I took a bite out of the sausage breakfast burrito that Joan had purchased for me. I then took the straw out of its white paper wrapping, and I placed it through the perforation in the lid of my small cup of orange juice. As I took a sip, I noticed something on the mahogany wood dining room table.

I covertly focused my eyes to examine it. Once I realized what it was, I started to choke on my orange juice. It was an imprint of Karen's backside. The mahogany wood made it very noticeable. I was able to make out the outline of both of Karen's butt cheeks. I could even decipher the part down the middle of them. The imprint was on the table, directly in the middle of where Joan and I were sitting.

Joan started to pat me on my back as I choked on my orange juice. I couldn't stop coughing. My eyes started to water as the choking intensified. Joan continued to pat me on my back. As I was in the middle of my coughing fit, I placed one of my hands on the linen placemat that was in front of me. I continued to cough as I guided the placemat over to the location of the imprint. I wiped the placemat over the butt imprint as I coughed and choked. Joan was so focused on making sure that I was alright that she didn't even notice. Eventually, I was able to collect myself. Joan gave me my orange juice cup so that I could take another sip.

"Are you okay?"

"Yeah, I'm fine. I guess my juice went down the wrong pipe."

Joan returned my placemat to its location. As she reorganized everything, I glanced over at the location where the imprint was before. It was just a big

218

smudge. There was nothing to be noticed. I took in a deep breath as I continued to enjoy my breakfast.

As I drove to work, my mind was filled with snapshots of Karen's bare image. I replayed our early morning actions over and over inside my head. It all happened so suddenly. I wondered what it was that made Karen drive over to my place and seduce me before going in to work. I also wondered if she was expecting something out of me. Did she break up with her fiancé? Was she expecting me to take his position? I tried to figure out Karen's perspective. As I drove through the crawling morning traffic, several thoughts and questions crammed my brain. What about Joan? We were just beginning to get serious, and I had cheated on her already. That is just pitiful. I shook my head back and forth as I felt disappointed in myself.

I attempted to clear my mind. I tuned my car radio to 96.3 so that I could listen to the *Russ Parr Morning Show*. It kept me laughing for the rest of my commute to work. As soon as I parked my car in the first available space in the parking garage, my cell phone started ringing. I looked at the screen on my BlackBerry and saw that it was Joan.

"Hello?"

"Hi, Tyson. Did you make it to work yet?"

"I just pulled into the parking garage that is about a block away from my building."

"That's good. I was just calling to make sure that you made it to work on time. I know that you have your presentation today. I also wanted to wish you luck. I know that you are going to do just fine. You have worked very hard on this account for some time now, and I am sure that the Weber people are going to be very impressed with all of your hard work."

"Thanks. I really appreciate that. Are you back on campus yet?"

"Yes. I just walked into one of the computer labs. I'm going to try to get a head start on some projects. It's going to be a long day for me. I can't wait until I graduate."

"I know the feeling. You don't have very long. You just have to tough it out. Well, I have to get going. I have two handfuls of things that I have to haul to the office for this presentation. I'll call you after we're done to let you know how things went."

"Okay. I'll talk to you later."

"Okay. Bye."

"Bye."

31 Tyson

I walked through the front doors of my office building and entered the lobby area. I smiled as I held the glass door open for one of the twenty-something female interns from my floor. She returned my smile as she exited the building. The security guard in the lobby area looked at me over the top of his wired reading glasses and nodded his balding head from behind the *Life* magazine that he was reading at his security desk. I returned the nod. I pressed the up arrow on the west wall of the lobby area, and I waited for the elevator to reach the main level. I reviewed my thoughts for our marketing presentation as I anxiously watched the highlighted numbers over the closed elevator doors decrease in value until the elevator reached the main level where I was waiting.

Once I stepped off the elevator, I headed straight for the conference room where the meeting was scheduled. We had about another thirty minutes before the meeting was scheduled to start. Inside my head, I continued to encourage myself. I had worked very hard on this account. I had worked many long hours to ensure that everything was done correctly. It was time to shine. The door to the conference room was open, and I could hear familiar voices as I approached the room. Karen was there, and she was going over a few things with our other team members. Everyone acknowledged me as I entered the conference room. Karen looked at me and flashed a blushing grin in my direction. She continued her conversation with our team members. I started to set up the projector for our presentation. I connected my Dell laptop to the PC input of the Sony LCD projector, which was located in the rear of the conference room. After that I went through my files on the hard drive of my laptop, and I selected the correct files that were needed for our presentation. I also logged onto the web page that we created for the Weber account. I then opened my PowerPoint slides and minimized them on the toolbar of my laptop. I was ready to get started.

Karen and I discussed a few things about our presentation before our managers and the Weber executives entered the room. We were the ones that were going to do most of the talking, so we wanted to make sure that we were both on the same page. We both avoided eye contact with each other as Karen and I discussed our plans for the account presentation. We all greeted both of the Weber execs as they entered the conference room. The woman looked to be in her late forties. She was tall with a slender physique. She was very attractive with dark skin and long, dark-brown hair. She was wearing a black, rounded-collar business suit with white pinstripes and a white, ruffled blouse. The woman's eyes were big and brown. I immediately noticed her perfectly arched eyebrows. The older man that was with her was wearing a blue suit with a white dress shirt and a red tie. The top of his head was bald, and the hair on the sides and the back of his head was white. The man's skin was pale with liver spots. He looked very knowledgeable and intimidating. Our manager walked into the conference room shortly after they did, wearing a black wrinkled suit and a dingy, white shirt with a black tie. Two other managers that I didn't recognize walked in behind him.

After the introductions were made, we began our presentation. I handed the laser pointer to Karen, and I took a step back. Karen started the presentation. She spoke with a manner of poise and comprehension that was unmatched. Karen continued to smile as all of the well-prepared statistics ran from her lips like rain drops from a leaf. I watched the Weber executives' facial expressions to see if they were buying what we were selling them. At times, during Karen's presentation, the man would smile and nod his head in approval of the data that were presented. The woman from Weber didn't show any facial expressions at all. She displayed her poker face during the entire meeting. Karen continued to speak. At times, the woman would ask Karen questions about a particular statistic that she spoke of. Karen didn't flinch. She was able to present the appropriate documents that supported her data.

A few minutes into Karen's presentation, she signaled for me to turn off the lights in the conference room. One of our team members pulled down the wall-mounted projector screen located at the front of the conference room so that Karen could show all her graphs and other information that was on my laptop, which was wired to the projector. Karen continued to speak. She used the laser pointer as she explained the graphical data that was in her presentation. After about ten slides of information, Karen passed the laser pointer to me, and she stepped out of the spotlight and into the shadows of the conference room.

I started my segment of the presentation to the Weber executives. This was also the final piece of the overall presentation. As I presented to the executives, it felt as though their eyes were burning into the fabric of my skin. I was very nervous, but I believe that I did a fine job of masking it. The information that I had previously rehearsed a million times before flowed out of my mouth. The longer that I presented my information, the more confident I became. I went over our radio advertisement ideas as well as our Internet and television advertisement ideas. I continued to stress to the Weber executives how important it was for us to have a strong Internet presence in this world of technology that we live in. I told them how vital it was for us to have a well-informed and user friendly website for the company. I observed the woman executive nod her head in accord with me. That added fuel to my flame of confidence. As I went on with my piece of the presentation, our manager looked on like a proud parent at his kid's soccer game. I could see the excitement in his face.

After I completed my part of the presentation, I felt like a weight was lifted from my shoulders. I was beyond relieved. We all shook hands, and my team thanked the two executives for giving us the opportunity to work with them. On his way out of the conference room, my manager shook my hand and patted me on my shoulder. He told me that I did a phenomenal job on my presentation. He also congratulated Karen and the other members of my team before leaving the conference room.

32 Tony

I finally got off Jay's couch the next day at six in the evening. Jay was at work, and I was still wearing the same clothes that I had on from the previous morning. I could smell the stench from my armpits. I smelled like an NFL linebacker. I needed a shower. I reached into the bag of my worldly possessions and pulled out a pair of jeans and a T-shirt. I then grabbed a fresh pair of boxers and socks out of my other bag and made my way to Jay's guest bathroom to take a shower.

After my shower, I got dressed and headed for the door. I didn't even bother to iron the clothes that I grabbed from my bag. My clothes were more wrinkled than an old lady in a swimming pool. I got into my car, and I began to drive. During my drive I fought to keep my mind clear, with little success. What was I going to do? I tuned the car radio to 106.7 to listen to the *Mo'Nique Show*. She made me laugh a little during my time of insanity. The rush hour traffic on Interstate 465 was thick. I swerved in and out of lanes to make my trip faster. After about an hour in traffic, I parked in front of Laura's townhome.

I didn't call Laura before I drove over there, so I was hoping she would be home. Half of me wanted her to be home. The other half was hoping that she wasn't. I got out of my car and made my way up her porch, and I rang the doorbell.

"Yes? Who is it?"

"It's Tony."

I heard Laura unlock the door. She opened the door with a look of bewilderment on her face.

"Tony. This is a surprise. What are you doing here?"

"I don't know. Is it alright if I come in?"

"Of course, come inside. You will have to excuse my appearance. I just got out of the shower. A few of my girlfriends and I are going to go and have some drinks tonight. I've only been home from work for about thirty minutes."

Laura had on a short, white terry robe. She was barefoot and shivering a little from the fall air rushing through the open door of her townhome. Laura quickly closed the door behind me after I entered her home.

"So, what's up? Is everything alright?"

"Not really. Karen and I broke up last night."

"I'm sorry to hear that. Are you alright?"

"Not really."

"What happened?"

"One of Karen's friends saw me leaving here the morning after you and I went out."

Laura showed concern. Her eyebrows rose, and her mouth dropped in shock from the information that I shared with her. She took a few steps backward without looking and sat on her couch. Her hand clinched the collar of her robe to ensure that it was closed. Laura rubbed her forehead with her other hand.

"Tony, I am so sorry. I didn't mean to—"

"Don't worry about it. It's not your fault. I shouldn't have come over here in the first place. As a matter of fact, I don't know why I am over here right now."

I started to walk toward the front door. As I reached for the door knob, Laura placed her hand on my forearm.

"Wait a minute. Are you mad at me? Tony, I didn't want you and your fiancé to break up. All I did was try to help you that night."

"Is that what you did? You were helping me?"

"Yes. I wasn't going to let you drive home drunk."

As we talked, I could feel myself becoming angry. I started to think about Karen. My chest became

228

tight. My breathing turned shallow as my heart began to beat hard and fast.

"What about all of those other days, Laura?"

"What are you talking about?"

"All of the lunches and the phone calls."

"Tony, you agreed to meet me, and you didn't have to answer the phone calls if you didn't want to. I didn't know that I was bothering you. I thought that you enjoyed eating lunch with me and talking with me on the phone. Let's not forget that you were calling me as well."

Laura's mood quickly changed as our conversation continued. I could see that I had hurt her feelings. I could hear it through the cracks in her voice. I circled the room as I continued to speak.

"That's the problem. I did like it, but that doesn't make it right. My life was just fine. My life was fine before I saw you in the bar that night. I was doing alright. I was in love and all set to get married. You had to come back, didn't you? You just had to come back. Why didn't you just stay in Texas? I thought that I had finally gotten over you until you came back."

Laura just sat there lifeless. Her face was stone. She didn't utter a word. Laura let me go on with my outburst.

"I was in love with you, Laura. I loved you more than any other woman that I had ever dated. I loved you more than I loved myself. You were my world. You left me. You left me without reason. Do you know what my life was like that year after you left me? It was terrible. I thought that I would never get over you. When you left Indianapolis, you took a part of me with you. I tried to date other women—I tried to love them—but I would always seem to find something wrong with them. I couldn't commit. Now that I think about it, I turned away some good women. I turned away women that had marriage potential. I broke up with women who would have done anything to keep me happy. It was just one thing that they couldn't be. They couldn't be you. I wanted them to be you, so it never worked out. I compared every one of them to you. Karen is a good woman. I love her very much. The sad thing is that I can't say that I love her with all of my heart because a piece of my heart is still with you. I hate that I love you."

I walked out of Laura's living room and into the kitchen. I leaned against the granite-topped center island. My eyes were locked to the floor. I couldn't possibly look at Laura after the words that I just aimed at her. I heard Laura get off the couch and make her way to the kitchen where I was. I didn't look up at her. I saw her feet walking closer to me. I finally looked up at her. She was standing right in front of me. Laura's face showed her pain. She stared at me. Neither of us spoke a single word. Laura then untied her terry robe. It opened a little in the front and exposed about a six-inch-wide vertical view. She wasn't wearing anything underneath the robe.

My eyes were fixed on the view that was just presented to me. Laura then slowly opened her robe and let it fall to the floor. She was completely naked. Laura shortened the distance between us. As she got closer to me, she wrapped her arms around me. I returned the gesture. We held each other. The bare skin on her back felt good to the palms of my hands. The scent from her recently washed body invaded my nostrils. I inhaled her fragrance. Laura looked up at me. We shared a gaze. She then pressed her lips against mine. The kiss was soft and tender. My lips parted and welcomed the taste of her mouth. We kissed. Her mouth was cool and wet. It was like eating a grape fresh out of the refrigerator. Laura's kisses satisfied my thirst. I could feel the reunion of our souls. I felt whole again.

My eyes opened slightly to glance at Laura. I wanted to make sure that it was real. Her eyes were closed, but her tears managed to escape her closed eyelids and saturate her lashes. I closed my eyes again as my own tears raced down my cheeks. As we kissed, I could taste the combination of our tears. It was fuel for our shared kiss. Our kiss became more intense. I had never experienced a kiss that emotional before. My mind started to think. I thought about how happy I used to be when Laura and I were to-gether. I thought about how sexy and attractive she was. The zipper of my jeans was holding on for dear life as my manhood pressed against it from the inside. Then, my mind started to think about Karen. I started to think about how much I loved Karen. I thought about the times that Karen was there for me when no other woman was. I thought about the future that I had promised to share with Karen. I instantly ended the kiss.

"I...We can't do this. I can't do this to Karen. I'm sorry. I have to go."

I eased my way out of the sandwich that was created by Laura and the center island in her kitchen. I bashfully covered the rise in my jeans as I rushed for the door. I didn't even look back at Laura. She didn't try to stop me. Once outside, I got into my car, and I drove off as fast as I could. After driving a few blocks, I pulled into the entrance of a nearby community. I pulled my car over to the curb, and I parked in front of a stranger's home. I placed the gear of my car into park, and I just sat there. I just sat there, and I cried like a baby. I couldn't stop the tears from falling. I felt alone. I was hurt. I was confused. I felt like my whole world was falling apart. I didn't know what to do. It was my fault. I brought it all on myself. I was the supplier of the downpour in my storm. There wasn't anyone I could blame. I placed both my hands over my eyes. They became drenched with my tears. I used the collar of my shirt to wipe away some of the tears, but more came.

I didn't want to go through it. I didn't want to face the consequences that were ahead of me. I knew deep inside that I had to make a choice. I was in love with two women, but I couldn't have them both. I knew that I would have to dedicate my heart to only one of them. I didn't want to make the selection. I cried harder. I struggled with the possibility that I might lose both women. I was weak. Every tear extracted something from me. How could I go on without Karen? Would I be able to continue to live without Laura? I was losing everything. I didn't want to work. I didn't want to talk. I didn't want to breathe. I didn't want to go on. I didn't have anyone I could go to. There wasn't anyone who could console me. It was times like these that a man needs his father's advice. I wanted so much to be able to pick up my cell phone and call my dad, but I couldn't. If he was still alive, then I'm sure he would have had some sound advice to give me that would help my situation. There was no one I could talk to.

The engine of my car was still running as music played through the radio's speakers. The sounds of Darius Brooks' gospel song "Your Will" started to play on the station that the radio was tuned to.

I opened my soggy eyes, and I gazed at the car radio. My chest continued to rise and fall. I wiped one side of my face. At that very moment, a feeling came over me. I didn't feel as alone anymore. I continued to listen to the words of that song. All of a sudden, I felt like praying. It had been so long since I had really prayed. It had been so long since I had been to a church service, but I felt like praying. I wiped the other side of my face. I sat up straight in the driver's seat of my car. I closed my eyes and I began to pray:

God, I know that it has been a while since I've prayed. I know that I haven't been to church in a long time. I also know that I have not been living as you would like me to. God, I am praying to you as a sinner. I am praying that you hear this sinner's prayer. I need you. My back is up against the wall. I don't have anywhere else to go. There isn't anyone I can talk to. I am lost. I am confused. I don't have the strength to carry on. I lost my girl and my home. I pray in the name of Jesus that you give me strength, God. I ask that you make me strong, even though I am feeling weak right now. It's not just about me choosing my mate. I am not satisfied with where I am in life right now. My job is good, but I want a career. I want my own business. I have been scared to continue to work on starting my business ever since my dad died. When he died, somehow I allowed my dreams to be buried with him. I miss my dad. God, you said that you would be a father to the fatherless. You said that you would supply all of my needs. I need you right now, Lord. I am in need of a blessing. I am praying to you for wisdom. I need wisdom to make the right decision. I need strength and courage to start my business. God, you already know the situation that I am going through with Laura and Karen. God, all I ask is that you lead me to the woman who is right for me. I ask that you point me in the right direction. God, even if neither of the women is for me, I will trust you. I place all of my problems and stress in your hands. I give it all up to you, God. I ask for wisdom, courage, and strength. It is in the name of Jesus that I pray, Amen.

33 Karen

I stood up from the table where I was sitting and raised my hand to get Stacey's attention. My coworkers and I were celebrating the successful completion of the Weber account at Jillian's, and I invited Stacey to join us. I was thankful that she could make it. Tyson and I had been avoiding contact with each other ever since our second encounter. Having Stacey there made me feel more at ease about being there.

Stacey walked over to our table, and we hugged. She sat in the empty chair that was next to mine. I introduced Stacey to all of my coworkers. After the formal introductions, Stacey and I immediately jumped into our own conversation.

"Thanks for coming."

"No problem, girl. You know that I'm not turning down any free drinks. You are still buying the drinks, right?"

"Yes, Stacey, the drinks are still on me like I told you."

We both laughed.

"So, how have you been handling everything?" Stacey asked.

"I'm still trying to cope with things. It's just a lot to handle. I miss him. I miss him very much. I just don't know if I can forgive him. I know that you had already told me about seeing Tony coming out of Laura's townhome that morning, but hearing it from his mouth was a reality check. He even admitted that he slept with her."

"Karen, you already knew that. I doubt that he would spend the night with his ex and nothing would happen. I know that it has been hard for you. You just have to do what is best for you."

"I know. It really hurts. I really miss him. I thought that things were going good for us. I just didn't want to believe that Tony would actually cheat on me. I mean, we have had a few fights, but nothing out of the ordinary. All of this has snatched my world right from underneath my feet. I feel lost. I feel like I don't know myself anymore."

As we talked, I fought to keep the tears from falling. Stacey held my hands to comfort me. She then motioned for the waitress to come over to our table. Stacey ordered a beer, and I ordered an apple martini. Stacey and I talked to each other the entire time. Everyone else at our table was having their own separate conversations. I glanced across the table at Tyson a few times during my conversations with Stacey. He didn't see me looking at him. He was holding his own conversation with one of the guys on our team.

Aside from all of the other obstacles that I was facing in my personal life, our presentation to the Weber executives and our managers was a success. Our work was approved and scheduled to be placed into action. The hard work that Tyson and I had put into this account finally paid off. Our managers were very pleased with us. My direct manager pulled Tyson and me aside and told us that he was thrilled at our performance on the account. He scheduled a Friday meeting with us to discuss our future with the company. I was very happy to hear that my hard work was not overlooked. Unfortunately, my contentment for my achievements at work was sidetracked by the recent events in my personal life. It was hard for me to take pleasure in my success at work, due to the failure of my relationship with Tony.

After about an hour of drinks and girl talk, I noticed Stacey looking past me at something that caught her attention. Her eyebrows wrinkled, and her eyelids squinted as she tried to get a better look at whatever it was that had distracted her. Then, she looked shocked. Stacey looked at me and showed concern.

"What? What's wrong, Stacey?"

"I don't want you to freak out, but I think that Laura is sitting at a table over on the other side of the bar area."

"Laura? You mean Tony's ex-girlfriend?"

"Yes."

"Where?"

"Right over there, by the air-hockey table."

I slowly turned to look in the direction that Stacey was referring to. I tried not to make it apparent that I was looking at her. I saw the table that Stacey was talking about, but I had never seen Laura before, so I didn't know which woman was her.

"Which one is Laura?"

"Laura is the one with the sandy brown hair."

A strange feeling came over me. I was looking across the room at the woman my fiancé cheated on me with. I was looking at a woman who has seen my man's body. She had felt his kisses. She knew what it was like to have him on top of her. Most of all, Tony was in love with her at one time. She was in love with him at one time also. They may still be in love with each other. I started to feel uncomfortable. I didn't know what to do. I didn't know how I should react. Stacey noticed my discomfort and started to stroke my arm to console me.

"I have to talk to her."

"Oh, we can do that. Let me just put my earrings in my purse. I just got them last week, and I don't want to lose them. I should probably leave my jacket here also. I plan on returning it tomorrow. You can focus on her. I think that I can handle her two friends who are with her."

"No. I didn't mean it like that, Stacey. I just want to talk to her. I want to know if it was more than a one-time thing between her and Tony."

I had to hold Stacey's arm to keep her from getting out of her chair. She was ready to go over to Laura's table and start a disturbance. I told her that I wanted to talk to Laura alone. I waited for a while. I saw Laura get up and walk over to the bar. This was the ideal time for me and Laura to talk without interference from any of our friends.

I walked over to the side of the bar where Laura was standing. As I got closer, I was able to get a better look at her. I was surprised at how professional she looked. I wasn't expecting that. Laura was a pretty woman. I could see how any man would be attracted to her. She looked like she was fresh out of a beauty salon. Her hair and makeup were both flawless. I am a woman with nice curves, but my body didn't compare to Laura's. Laura was wearing a long-sleeve, black, cascading ruffle dress that stopped just below her knees. The v-neck of the dress showed just a hint of cleavage, while the rest of the dress tastefully boasted just how physically fit Laura was. Her waist was small, and her hips were curvy. Laura was wearing a pair of black high heel pumps with a metal Gucci crest on the front of each shoe. I tried to get her attention.

"Excuse me. Is your name Laura?"

She looked at me as if she was trying to figure out who I was.

"Yes. My name is Laura."

"Hello, Laura. My name is Karen."

The change in Laura's mood was noticeable. She tensed up a little as if she were preparing for a squabble.

"Don't worry. I didn't come over here to start anything with you. I just want to talk to you. Nice shoes, by the way."

"Thank you."

"I'll buy the next round of drinks for you and your girls if you'd have a conversation with me."

"Sure. I don't see any harm with that."

Laura ordered drinks for her and her friends. I paid the bartender while she took the drinks over to the table that she was sharing with her friends. After Laura delivered the spirits to her table of friends, she met me at a small, unoccupied table near the bar. She placed her drink on the table where I was sitting, and then she sat across the table from me. She crossed her legs and took a sip of her drink.

Why did she have to go after my man? My mind was all over the place. I wanted to go off on her. I wanted to scream at her like a wild woman. I wanted to grab a handful of that sandy brown hair and pull until it separated from her scalp. But I realized that Laura was not the one to blame. Laura didn't make any commitments to me. Laura was not the one who was dishonest. She didn't owe me anything. It was Tony that I should be mad at. Tony was the one who abused my trust. He was the one who was thinking with the wrong brain. It was possible that Tony lied to Laura just as he did to me.

"Thank you for agreeing to talk to me."

"No problem. I must admit that it is kind of strange to be sitting across the table from Tony's girlfriend."

"Fiancée."

"Oh, no disrespect intended. I just didn't see a ring on your hand."

We both looked down at my ring finger after Laura's statement. I knew that she said it to get to me, but I let it go. I could tell that Laura was just as uncomfortable talking to me as I was with her.

I continued: "Laura, I mean this with all due respect. I just want you to tell me the truth. I know that you don't owe me anything, but I'm just asking for the truth. I'm not here to start any trouble. We are both beautiful, professional women, and I think that we should be able to have a respectful conversation."

"I agree. I apologize for my comment. I just didn't know what to expect from you, so I guess that I was a little on edge about the situation."

"Understood and apology accepted."

"So, Karen, what is it that you want to know?"

I came straight to the point: "How long have you and Tony been messing around?"

Laura sat up straight in her chair. She took a sip of her drink. Laura then placed both of her elbows on the table, folded her hands together, and inhaled deeply.

"Tony didn't cheat on you."

I was annoyed. I could not believe that she would lie to me after I just bought her and her greedy girlfriends drinks. She must have thought that I was dumb. I knew that she was just trying to take up for Tony.

"Laura, I know that you and Tony went out that night. I also know that Tony spent the night with you. One of my girlfriends saw him leave your town-home early that morning."

"Let me guess. It was probably the girl that is over at your table staring at me as if I stole something from her."

I looked over at the table where Stacey was sitting. Stacey looked like a Doberman on a leash. She was waiting for the word for her to jump. I think that she was actually foaming at the mouth.

"Don't pay her any attention. She is just a little protective of me."

"Karen, we did go out that night, but nothing happened."

"Forgive me for saying this, but I find that very hard to believe."

"I know, it sounds crazy, but nothing happened. I called Tony, and I asked him if he wanted to come with me to see my friend's band play. He accepted. Tony came and picked me up at my townhome, and we headed to the club where the band was playing. While we were at the club, Tony had more than a few drinks. We talked and listened to the band play. After a few hours, Tony was inebriated out of his mind. I had to help him walk to the car. Of course I had to drive us back to my townhome because I rode with him. I told him that he was welcome to stay in my guest room and sober up, and that is where he stayed."

"So, are you trying to tell me that the two of you did not have sex that night?"

"That is exactly what I am telling you. I will say that I did fall asleep in the guest room with him, but nothing happened. I was keeping an eye on him in case he got sick in the middle of the night. We were both fully clothed."

"Did you kiss him?"

"Not that night. All that we did was hug each other a few times, but that was the extent of it."

"When you said that you didn't kiss him that night, does that mean that the two of you kissed on another night?"

Laura was unable to hide how uncomfortable my question made her. She paused for a while before answering the question.

"Tony came by my townhome this evening a little after I had gotten home from work. He was no-ticeably upset. Tony told me about what happened between the two of you. He basically blamed me for everything that was happening between you two. It wasn't until then that I was reminded of how much I care for Tony. Seeing him hurt like that for another woman did something to me. I realized then that I still love Tony. I couldn't help it. I kissed him. I made the move on him. Although Tony did kiss me back, he stopped it short and left. He told me that he couldn't cheat on you. Tony really loves you Karen. You have a good man. Tony made a mistake. It's you that he wants to be with, not me. Don't make the same mistake that I did. I would give up everything to be in your position. Don't let him slip away from you."

Laura stood up from the table where we were sitting. She blinked a few times to stop the tears that were forming in her eyes.

"I think I've given you all of the information that you need. It was nice to meet you. Thank you for the drinks."

Laura walked away. And then it hit me. Tony wasn't the one who cheated. I was the cheater. Although Tony did end up kissing Laura, it was after we had broken up. No doubt, he should not have gone out on a date with Laura, but he didn't have sex with her. He didn't even kiss her. Laura didn't have any reason to lie to me. She could have easily lied and told me that they had sex, but she didn't. Why would Tony admit to doing something that he didn't do?

I started to feel light-headed. What had I done? I broke up with Tony for nothing. I also had sex with another man. I allowed another man to enter a place that was reserved for Tony and Tony alone. To make things even more messed up, I cheated on Tony with the very person that he had assumed I was cheating with in the first place. I felt like the biggest tramp in Indianapolis.

In a matter of minutes, I was transformed from the victim into the bad guy. I cheated on my fiancé. I felt awful. I immediately grabbed my phone and tried to call Tony. His phone was turned off, so it went directly to his voicemail. I left a message informing him to call me as soon as he checked his messages. I made several attempts to call him after that without any success. My heart was beating rapidly.

I walked over to the table where Stacey and the rest of my coworkers were sitting. I tried to ignore the fact that Tyson was sitting at the table, even though I could feel his eyes on me. I told Stacey that I was leaving.

"Is everything alright? What's wrong?"

"Nothing. I just have to go."

I walked out of Jillian's as fast as I could. I was almost running. I was trying to beat my tears to the door. As soon as I made my way outside the building, the tears began to flow from my eyes and down the sides of my face. I just stood there and covered my face. I was crying out of control. I was hysterically walking around in circles. I couldn't believe what was happening to me. Most of all, I couldn't believe what I let happen to me. I allowed myself to become a person that I despised. I had compromised my body and my principles. Most of all, I was the one who had gambled our relationship, not Tony. I tried to call Tony's phone again without any success. Flashbacks of my second encounter with Tyson danced around inside my memory. I shook my head, hoping that the thoughts would fall out of one of my ears. They remained. Pictures of Tyson's bare chest flashed across my mind. Visions of me positioned on Tyson's dining room table played inside my head. My transgressions haunted me. I just started walking down Meridian Street with both of my hands grabbing my hair. People stared at me as I walked by them. I just continued to walk without a destination.

Before I knew it, I had walked a few blocks. I was standing on the grand steps of the monument at Monument Circle. I sat on one of the steps of the monument and just stared at the cobblestone street.

What have I done?

I continued to recite that question over and over to myself. I buried my head into my hands, and I continued to cry. I could hear the sound of people walking by. I could hear the sound of cars making their way around the curved street of Monument Circle. I didn't look up. I was ashamed at what I had done. I felt like everyone who saw me sitting on that step was aware of what I had done. Regret and shame occupied the empty space inside my soul. As I was

248

sitting on that step, Stacey continued to call my cell phone. I allowed her calls to go to my voicemail.

Tyson also called my cell phone while I was at Monument Circle. I'm sure that he noticed how upset I was when I left Jillian's. I definitely didn't have a desire to address him at that moment. I wiped the tear and mascara mix from my face with both my hands. I pressed both my knees together, and I wrapped my arms around them. I continued to shake my head as the motion picture of what I had done continued to play inside my head.

34 Tony

I didn't sleep much last night. I had lots on my mind. I awoke at about seven in the morning to the sound of Jay's getting ready for work. I didn't sit up from my location on Jay's couch. I stared at the ceiling as thoughts rushed through my head. I could hear Jay's footsteps entering the living room where I was situated.

"Are you going to work today?" he asked.

"I wasn't planning on it. I'm going to call in and let them know that I am not feeling well."

"Man, you haven't gone to work all week. Aren't you afraid of losing your job?"

"At this point, I really don't care. It seems as if I am losing everything nowadays."

I could read the frustration in Jay's face as he spoke to me. He started to rub his head like he always does when he's got something to say.

"Tony, can I be honest with you?"

"Sure. Go ahead."

"Look. You can't keep beating yourself up like this. I know that things are bad right now, but you can't let it beat you. It doesn't make any sense for you to throw away everything that you have worked hard for. You messed up. You lost your girl because you messed up. You made a mistake, but you can make it right. Karen is a good girl. Most of all, she is a great person. I know that I always laugh at you and give you a hard time whenever you do nice things for her, but she deserves it. She makes you happy. Karen is marriage material. I would do anything and everything to have a girl like that. Any man would. The question is, would you do anything and everything to get her back? If Karen is who you really want, you should do everything within your power to win her back. If that doesn't work, then you do more. Notice that I said win her back and not get her back. Anyone can get something, but in order to win something, you have to work for it. If she is the one you want to spend the rest of your life with, go and win her back. If it's Laura you want, then you have to do everything within your power to show her that you love her and that you want to be with her for the long haul. Laura didn't leave you because she wasn't in love with you anymore. She left you because she felt that you were unsure about your feelings toward her and your future together. Don't just lie here and sulk. Do some-

251

thing about it. This is your time to make things better. If you want to be with Laura, now you have the perfect opportunity to do so. I don't care which woman you choose. Just get out there and win the one that you really want."

Jay grabbed his jacket from the coat closet in the living room, and he left. I sat for a while and thought about what Jay had said. He was right. I couldn't just sit there and let my woman slip away from me. I had to fight to win my girl. I had to fight to win my life back. I immediately got off Jay's couch and ran to the bathroom to take a shower and get dressed.

An hour later, I was parking my car in a downtown parking garage. I got out of my car and headed for the main level Illinois Street exit of the parking garage. I was equipped with my love for Karen in my chest and a dozen roses in my hand that I had picked up on my way downtown. I was focused on the dialog that I would use to convince Karen to take me back. As I made my way to Washington Street, I could hear the sound of a saxophone's melody. As I crossed the street underneath the Arts Garden, I soon discovered the source of the smooth tunes.

A homeless man was playing his saxophone on the corner of Illinois and Washington. He was wearing a long, dirty overcoat and torn jeans. His gray hair was matted, and his beard was long and nappy. Several people walked by him as he played his version of B. B. King's "Blues Man" on his sax. I easily recognized the song because it was one of my favorites. After I crossed the street and arrived at the corner where he was playing, I stood there for a moment and listened. I was the only one who had paused to listen. As the sax man played his tunes, the many familiar noises of downtown Indianapolis seemed to disappear. I didn't hear any cars going by or any individual conversations in my ear as people walked by me. All I could hear were the smooth tunes from his saxophone.

As the man played, his eyes were closed. He even appeared to be smiling as he was playing. He was really into it. I don't even think that he noticed me standing there. After he ended the piece that he was playing, the man looked up at me. He smiled and nodded.

"'Blues Man,' right?"

"That's right, young man. I see that you are a young man who knows his music."

The man seemed happy that he had someone to talk to. I could only imagine how many people pass him by on a single day without saying a word to him.

"How long have you been playing the saxophone?"

"I've been playing since I was ten."

"I can tell. It sounds like you have some experience at it."

I was intrigued by the guy. I wondered how a homeless person could seem so cheerful. I wondered what it was that made him smile. He was even smiling as we talked. In the middle of all his needs and circumstances, this homeless guy was able to smile. Here I was lying up depressed from a breakup and not showing up for work, but this homeless man was able to find joy in a situation far worse than mine.

"Sir, can I ask you a question?"

"Sure, young man. Anything you like."

"I noticed that you appeared to be smiling as you played. Is it because playing the saxophone makes you happy?"

"I guess you can say that. There is a lot more to it than that. Playing this old sax just gives me good memories."

The man smiled and looked up at the sky as he said that.

"That's understandable. If you don't mind my asking, how did you become homeless?"

The man stopped looking at the sky and focused his attention on me. He walked over to the building we were standing in front of, and he leaned his back against it. He was still smiling. He motioned

254

for me to stand on the wall next to him so that we weren't in the way of any pedestrians trying to walk by us.

"Young man, about twenty years ago, I was just like you. I had a good-paying job, nice clothes, and even a nice car. I had a wife and a home. I even had a child from a previous relationship before my wife. Everything was going great. I was working over at the Chrysler plant. I left home one morning with a job, and I came back an hour later without one. The plant started to lay people off, and I was in the first wave of layoffs. My wife still had her job, and I was able to collect unemployment checks for a while. Then, my wife's job let her go, and the unemployment checks ran out. Times became very rough for us. My parents died when I was young, and I don't have any siblings. My wife had a large family, but they didn't care for me very much. You see, my wife and I married very young without the approval of her family. Her family offered to help her out as long as she left me. She refused. My wife never left my side."

The man's smile grew larger as he talked about his wife. It was easy to notice that he really loved his wife.

"We lost everything," he continued. "We lost our home, the car, and all of our accounts were dried up. We were unable to find employment, and there wasn't anyone who could help us. My wife could have left me to stay with one of her family members, but she didn't. She never even brought it up. She lived on the streets with me, and she loved me. My wife loved to hear me play. She said that it reminded her of our first date at an old blues bar in Chicago. My wife lived on the street with me for ten years. She never left my side. Everyone else did, but she stayed with me. I even lost contact with my daughter because her mother moved out of state."

"What happened to your wife?"

"She passed away. We had a bad winter, and she caught pneumonia. That was five years ago. I've been on the streets for fifteen years. I miss her dearly."

"So, is that why you smile? Is it because you are thinking of you wife?"

"Son, I smile because I have experienced something that many people die without ever seeing. I experienced true love. God allowed me to know what true love feels like. He blessed me with a woman who loved me no matter what. I had a woman who took her vows to heart. She had several opportunities to leave me, but she didn't. She had my back until she took her very last breath. She never talked down to me, even while we were sleeping in dirty alleys and using cardboard for blankets. That woman continued to encourage me. I may be without a lot of things, but I am not without love. You see, son, God is love. So, if you experience true love, then you are experiencing God. Love can't be duplicated, and love can't be impersonated. Sometimes it takes your losing everything to realize that you didn't need it in the first place. When you don't have anything, you seem to appreciate what's left. Son, I am happy. I have been homeless for fifteen years, and I am still here. At night, I still get on my knees in whatever alley it is that I am sleeping in, and I thank God for my life and the love of my life."

I was speechless. I felt like my eyes had been opened for the first time in my life. I looked down the street at the building where Karen worked, and then I looked at the homeless guy. I handed him the dozen roses that I had bought for Karen.

"Here. I want you to stop by the cemetery and place these on your wife's grave site."

After that, I turned and started to walk back across the street to the parking garage. I had a renewed feeling inside of me. Listening to the homeless guy made me realize that it wasn't Karen whom I was truly in love with. I was in love with Laura. Laura didn't leave me before because she didn't want to be with me anymore. She left because she couldn't stand to see me with another woman. I was being young and dumb. I was too young to appreciate the love that I had at that time. Before I entered the parking garage, I looked back across the street where the homeless guy was playing the saxophone before. To my surprise, he was gone. I looked both directions down the street to see if he was walking, but I didn't see any sign of him. I grinned, and then I entered the parking garage.

35 Tony

I drove my car out of the parking garage, and I headed for the interstate. It was after ten in the morning, and I figured that Laura was at work. My cell phone's battery was drained, so I was unable to call her. What I had on my mind could not wait until she got off from work. I had to tell her how I felt. I weaved in and out of the morning traffic on Interstate 65. I accelerated my rate of speed at every given opportunity.

After thirty minutes of driving like a madman, I pulled into the Verizon parking lot in Fishers. I parked my car in the first available spot that caught my eye. I immediately darted for the entrance of the building. I was out of breath when I got to the receptionist's counter in the main lobby of the building. A slim-faced woman with straight, blonde hair sat at the desk behind the counter.

"May I help you?"

"Yes. My name is Tony, and I'm here for Laura Statton."

"Alright, just one moment please."

The slim-faced receptionist raised the receiver of her telephone to her ear and began to dial Laura's extension. I noticed her talking to someone on the other end of the line, but I couldn't make out the conversation. Shortly after that, the slim-faced receptionist placed the receiver back on its base.

"I just spoke with Ms. Statton's secretary, and she informed me that Ms. Statton is in a meeting right now. Would you like to wait for her?"

"How long is the meeting?"

"She didn't say. You can leave a message for her if you'd like."

"What floor is she on again?"

"The fifth, but—"

Before the slim-faced lady could complete her sentence, I sprinted in the direction of the stairway. I could hear the receptionist in the background yelling at me to stop. I could also hear her getting the attention of the security guard who was in the lobby area. When I reached the doorway to the stairway, I looked back at the receptionist area and witnessed two flabby security guards running toward my direction. Without more ado, I entered the stairway and dashed up the many stairs that led to the fifth floor. As I made my way up to the fifth floor, one floor at a time, I could hear the heavy breathing from the unexercised security guards behind me.

By the time I made it to the fifth floor, I was fatigued. I barely had enough energy to open the door to the stairway to enter the hall of the fifth floor. My movements slowed as I entered the hallway. My energy was spent. I rested my hands on my knees and tried to catch my breath. To my surprise, one of the security guards swung open the stairway door. It caught me off guard. I fell to the ground in my surprise. He was sweating like George W. Bush at Black Expo. Luckily for me, he was too tired to grab me at that moment. I picked myself up off the floor and ran to the entrance of the offices that were located on that level.

"Stop!"

"Freeze!"

I could hear the yelling from both security guards in the hallway. Apparently, everyone else could hear them also. When I entered the office area, everyone was standing up from their desks and looking in my direction. I ran to the nearest cubical.

"Where is Laura Statton's desk?"

The older lady was too afraid to answer. Soon after that, my two security guard friends from the lobby came running into the office area.

"I said freeze!"

"Stop right there!"

For some reason, their words just didn't sound too convincing as they waved flashlights at me. I tried to continue my journey through the office.

"Where is she? Laura! Can someone find her for me? Please."

The security guards finally got close enough to grab me. I wrestled with them to free myself, but both of them were too strong. You could see the concern on the other employees' faces while all of this was going on.

"Let me go! I didn't do anything! I just want to talk to her!"

"Tony? Is that you? What is going on? Let him go. It's alright." Laura had come out in the midst of the commotion.

I looked up from the submission hold that the two unintimidating security guards had me in. Laura was standing in the doorway of what appeared to be a conference room. Everyone was staring at me like I was crazy.

"I said let him go!"

The security guards obeyed her command. I gave them a look as if I could take them both.

"Tony. What's going on? What is wrong with you?"

"I'm sorry for all of this. I just had to talk to you."

"What could be so important that you think you have to break into my office building?"

"I just wanted to talk to you, and they wouldn't let me."

I was out of breath. My words were slurred, and I was sweating just as hard as my security friends. Everyone in the office still had their attention focused on me.

"Well, here I am. What is it?"

I was breathing heavily and clinching my chest.

"I...I talked to this homeless dude, and... and...and...He was in love."

"What homeless dude? Tony, what are you talking about?"

"They...slept under boxes...and he played his saxophone."

"What? Tony. You sound crazy. Take a deep breath."

I tried to get my breathing back in rhythm. I took a few deep breaths like Laura had recommended. Laura left her location in the doorway of the conference room and started to walk closer to where I was. Everyone was still staring at us.

"Everything that has been going on lately has had me baffled. I was torn between you and Karen. I was mad that you came back to Indianapolis and confused things for me. I was on my way to Karen's job to try to get her back. I was sure that she was the one for me. Then, I ran into this homeless guy on the street. This man explained to me what true love is. Love is not convenient. It's not something that you plan. It just happens. You can't force it. When it is really true love, it just kind of fits into place, like a puzzle. With all of that said, love is not easy. It takes work. Just like that puzzle. If you turn it upside down, then the puzzle falls apart, and you have to start all over again, but that doesn't mean that it wasn't true love. It just means you have to learn to appreciate it more."

Laura's eyes began to fill with tears. She tried to keep a straight face in front of her peers.

"What is it that you are attempting to say, Tony?"

"What I'm trying to say is that I love you. Laura, I have loved you for as long as I can remember. When we were together, things weren't perfect. We had our fights and our disagreements, but every relationship does. If a relationship doesn't have some kinds of disagreements, then it's not real. It's a fairy tale. It's the fights, the disagreements, and the storms

264

that test the bond of your relationship. I was just too young to appreciate what it was that we had. When you left, I was miserable. Like I told you before, you took a part of me with you. When we reconnected, it felt just like that, a reconnection. I felt like that piece of me that I knew I was missing had been returned. I thought that I was in love with Karen. I thought that I had loved other women before you also, but it wasn't until now that I realized it wasn't love. I have loved only one person, and that person is and always will be you. I don't have the capacity to love another woman. I don't want to. All I want is you. I don't care about anything else in this world. I thank God for the day that I met you."

I turned my attention to a nearby desk. I rummaged through one of the drawers. I grabbed a paper clip out of one of the drawers. I hurried to change it from its original shape to form a circle. I walked over to Laura, and I dropped to one knee.

"You are the love of my life. I was placed on this earth to love you. With you, I am everything. Without you, I am nothing. Laura, will you do me the honor of being my friend, my partner, my dream girl, and my wife?"

Laura covered her face with both her hands. She then removed her hands and showed the most beautiful smile that I had ever seen. Her face was full of tears, and she was nodding her head up and down.

"Yes. Yes, I will be all of that for you."

The office erupted in applause and cheers. Laura allowed me to place my homemade paper clip engagement ring on her finger. She then helped me off the floor and wrapped her arms around my neck. We kissed as the sound of cheers and applause got even louder. After our kiss, we continued to hold each other. I was smiling from ear to ear. While I was holding Laura, my eyes scanned the room. Everyone who was in the office area with us had tears in their eyes. Even the two security guards that chased me up those flights of stairs were crying. My neck was still sore from the chokehold that they placed me in, but I was okay with it, as long as they didn't have me arrested.

36 Tyson

I got out of bed around six in the morning. I barely got any sleep last night. I was excessively excited about my promotion review meeting that was scheduled for today. I felt like a kid on Christmas Eve. During my moments of unrest throughout the night, I occasionally would look over at Joan sleeping on the other end of the bed. She looked extremely peaceful as she slept. While I was in the shower, I could smell the aroma of coffee brewing downstairs.

After my shower, I continued to get ready for work. I had on my black suit that I picked up from the cleaners over the weekend. My white dress shirt was bright and starched to perfection. As I was tying my red tie, I could hear Joan calling me to eat breakfast. I made my way downstairs and entered the kitchen. Joan was still in her night clothes. She had on a black camisole and matching boy-shorts. Her ensemble made me a witness of how beautiful her body was. Although she was slim, every curve was in the right place. I walked over to Joan and kissed her on the back of her neck. She smiled and touched the side of my face.

"Thanks for making me breakfast."

"You're welcome, handsome. I wanted to make sure that you had a full stomach on your big day."

"I'm very nervous. I don't know if I'll be able to keep my food down. I might puke all over the conference table."

"I am sure that you will be just fine."

I sat at the table as Joan poured fresh coffee into two cups. She placed one cup on the table in front of where she was going to sit, and she placed the other cup in front of me. She kissed me on my forehead.

"This is what you've worked so hard for. Just think about the long days and late nights that you have spent at that office. This is your time to harvest the benefits of all of it."

Joan was right. I had worked long and hard for this moment. I drank my coffee and ate about a quarter of the meal that was prepared for me. Joan didn't have to go to class, so I told her that she could hang out at the loft until I got home from work. We had plans to go out and celebrate. She gave me a big kiss and escorted me to the door.

I arrived at work ready for my meeting. Karen and I were scheduled for the same meeting time. Since we were the main instruments on the Weber account, we were the ones my manager wanted to meet with. He told me earlier in the week that he wanted to go over our future direction with the company. He also told me that the entire management staff was impressed with the outcome of the account. I sat at my desk for a few minutes to get my anxiety under control. I read a few of my e-mails, and then I headed for the conference room for my meeting.

As I walked down the hall to the conference room, I had a renewed sense of confidence. For once in my corporate career, I felt like I was finally about to get what I deserved. All of my education and experience was finally going to propel me to the next altitude of corporate America. I walked with my chest out and my head high.

Karen was already in the conference room, which did not surprise me at all. Karen and our manager were already engaged in a conversation. Both of them greeted me as I entered the room. I took my assigned place next to Karen on one side of the table. My manager sat on the other side of the table.

"First off, I would like to thank the both of you for all of your hard work. If it weren't for the two of you, I don't think that we would have been able to pull this project off. I know that I was on the both of you pretty tough, but you managed to keep your heads. You handled this project as professionals.

Tyson, you have been here with us for many years. Your accomplishments are unmatched. Karen, you have truly stepped up within the past year, and everyone here has noticed."

Both Karen and I smiled as we basked in the praises from our manager. Karen and I hadn't said much to each other since our get-together in the parking lot earlier this week. It would be safe to say that we'd both been avoiding each other. We both listened as our manager continued.

"It is because of your hard work that I took up for the two of you. I convinced all of the other managers to allow you to bow out gracefully."

Confusion filled my thoughts. I looked over at Karen, and I could see the same confusion on her face.

"Bow out gracefully? What are you talking about?" I said.

Our manager stood up from his seat on the other side of the conference table. He walked over to the other side of the conference room without saying another word. He then turned on the LCD television that was mounted on the south wall of the room and pressed play on the DVD player located just below it. Karen grabbed both sides of her face with her hands. Her face instantly turned red, and her eyes soon followed. Tears flowed out of her eyes like water into a glass. Karen shook her head back and forth continuously. Her lips formed words, but nothing came out of her mouth.

There it was. The LCD television on the wall showed a security recording of us having sex in the company lot. Although the recording was in black and white, it was very clear. One could easily make out the two individuals performing in the closed-circuit television porno. To make things even worse, it was recorded on the side of the car where all of the events took place. From the video, it seemed as if the hidden security camera was right above the spot Karen had parked that day. In the video, Karen was draped over the trunk of the car, and I was standing behind her, stroking away. The recording was so clear that you could see the dimples in my butt cheeks as I performed my moves.

I couldn't speak. I couldn't move. My eyes were glued to the television. It felt like a nightmare. In my mind, I prayed that it was a nightmare. I was waiting for someone to wake me up from this terrible dream. I thought, someone pinch me, bite me, kick me, or something. This could not be happening. My stomach began to turn. My throat tightened as my mouth watered.

"I have prepared a resignation for the both of you. I was able to convince management to allow you to receive your pensions upon your resignation. I just need both of you to sign right h—"

I couldn't hold it any longer. All of the muscles within my body just let go. All of a sudden, I puked. I tried to turn from the table, but it went everywhere. Karen got the worst of it. I couldn't stop it. I felt like I was starring in the remake of *The Exorcist*. I puked on Karen, the conference room table, the floor, and myself. The food that Joan had made me for breakfast was now on display for everyone to see. I think that I even saw a piece of sausage on the collar of Karen's blouse. Karen cried and screamed in harmony. She stood there with her arms stretched from her sides with my puke all over her. It was even in her hair.

My manager moved back from the table just in time. He looked as if he had just seen a ghost. His mouth dropped as he looked at Karen. They both looked at me like I was out of my mind. Awkwardness filled the room. I was mortified.